DOVER
STRIKES
AGAIN

DOVER STRIKES AGAIN

Joyce Porter

A Foul Play Press Book

The Countryman Press, Inc.
Woodstock, Vermont

This edition first published in 1991 by Foul Play Press,
an imprint of The Countryman Press, Inc.,
Woodstock, Vermont 05091

ISBN 0-88150-211-1

Printed in the United States of America

10 9 8 7 6 5 4 3 2 1

To David Aubrey Cuttill, with humble affection

Of course Superintendent Underbarrow shouldn't have been standing on this station platform at all, not by rights he shouldn't. It wasn't his job to act as a one-man welcome committee to a couple of blooming detectives. He was uniformed branch himself, and proud of it. Somebody from the plain-clothes mob should have been doing this. Or the chief constable himself, if it came to that. The trouble was they'd all got cold feet. Superintendent Underbarrow chuckled softly to himself. Aye, cold feet! As if these murder squad chaps weren't as human as the rest of us. All right – so everything hadn't exactly been done according to Cocker. These fellows would understand the difficulties – wouldn't they? – and muck in like everybody else had done. Superintendent Underbarrow chuckled again. Muck in? That was an apt phrase if ever he'd coined one !

With a hoarse scream the express came pounding into the station but Superintendent Underbarrow stood his ground quietly and confidently. If the first-class carriages didn't stop directly opposite him, he'd eat his hat.

The quiet confidence was fully justified. The train rocked to a halt and a second or two later one of the first-class carriage doors opened. Superintendent Underbarrow watched placidly as a handsome young man struggled out on to the platform with a couple of heavy suitcases. Apart from a middle-aged lady up at the front, nobody else was alighting from the train. A faint frown creased Superintendent Underbarrow's cheerful features and he examined the young man more closely. Suede boots, pink shirt and a camel-hair overcoat that had cost sixty guineas if it had cost a penny. He looked more like one of those la-di-da male models than a decent, hard-working copper.

The handsome young man turned back to the train and began lugging out yet a third suitcase. Superintendent Underbarrow's face cleared. The murder bag or he was a Dutchman!

The handsome young man still hadn't finished. He was now assisting an older, bigger and uglier man down on to the platform and getting heartily cursed for his pains in the process.

Superintendent Underbarrow relaxed. Ah, this was more like it! One of the old school, this! Bowler hat, scruffy black boots and a face to match! Superintendent Underbarrow began to move forward.

The porter skipped merrily along the train, slammed the door shut and flashed a two-fingered signal to the guard. The diesel motors cut down to a soft purr and the train pulled smoothly away.

The handsome young man turned as Superintendent Underbarrow approached and then stiffened to attention. 'Superintendent Underbarrow, sir? I'm Detective-Sergeant Mac-Gregor, sir, from the Yard. And this' – he stepped aside so that the superintendent could get a clear view – 'is Detective Chief Inspector Dover.'

To Superintendent Underbarrow's eternal credit, the hesitation was only momentary. He checked his involuntary gulp in mid-swallow, tacked his smile of welcome back on his face and held out his hand.

Chief Inspector Dover ignored it. 'It's raining,' he said.

The remark was not a conversational gambit. It was an impeachment.

Superintendent Underbarrow found himself stammering out an apology for the local weather but it was already too late. Chief Inspector Dover's back, as he lumbered off down the platform, was unresponsive and unappeased.

By the time they had all crowded into the waiting police car, the superintendent had recovered some of his faith in human nature. 'Well now,' he began, 'did you have a good journey?'

There was a contemptuous sniff from the back seat beside him but Sergeant MacGregor showed that he, at least, had got some manners.

He turned round in his place beside the driver. 'Very good, thank you, sir.'

Superintendent Underbarrow beamed gratefully at him. 'I'm afraid we've got a sticky one lined up for you this time,' he went on, with slightly more cordiality than he would have shown to one of his own sergeants.

'So we've gathered, sir.'

Superintendent Underbarrow grinned. 'An earthquake, eh? I'd never have expected that if I'd tried with both hands, not in a thousand years I wouldn't. And in Sully Martin, too! I mean, it's such a sleepy little place. Well, they've hit the headlines this time and no mistake. By the way,' – he put the question casually – 'did you happen to catch me on the telly, eh?'

'I'm afraid not, sir. They interviewed you, did they?'

'Yes – a couple of times on both channels as a matter of fact. Shocking waste of time when you're up to your ears trying to cope but that's the way things are these days. The chief constable had overall control, of course – major disaster and all that sort of thing – but the transport was my pigeon. As things turned out transport was the key to the whole business.'

'Really, sir?'

'Oh, yes.' Superintendent Underbarrow leaned forward. 'Still is, if it comes to that. We've not broken the back of the problem yet.' He glanced out of the side window. 'And we shan't, not until this dratted rain stops. You see, it's the main road running up to Sully Martin that's the trouble. There's nearly a quarter of a mile of it that's just disappeared.'

'Goodness me!' MacGregor was getting a crick in the back of his neck but, since Dover had now got his eyes closed and his mouth open, the burden of social intercourse had to be shouldered by someone.

'Secondary effect of the earthquake,' explained Superintendent Underbarrow with a knowing nod. 'Sully Martin's stuck up on a hill, you understand, and the first tremors virtually cracked it clean in two. One corner of the village – the bit up on the cliff overhanging the main road – just sort of broke off and slid down the hillside. The road was buried under an avalanche of mud and houses and cars and sheds and goodness knows what. You've never seen such a mess and we can't get it shifted. As soon as the bulldozers scoop up one loadful, another lot comes sliding down and takes its place. And, apart from a couple of cart tracks, this road's the only way into Sully Martin from any direction. You can imagine what it's like trying to do rescue work in the village itself. We can't get any heavy equipment up there.'

'How awful,' said MacGregor.

'Mind you,' – Superintendent Underbarrow spoke rather bitterly for him – 'there's no shortage of unsolicited advice. I even had the chief constable sticking his oar in this morning. Still, I let him have it straight. "If you think somebody else can make a better job of," I told him, "they're welcome to try. Don't you bother about my feelings," I said. "I'm not one of your . . ."' Superintendent Underbarrow had intended to fling himself back in his seat to underline the indignation he felt but Chief Inspector Dover's amorphous bulk had somehow oozed across and was now occupying all the available space. Superintendent Underbarrow gazed in astonishment at this remarkable occurrence and then glanced up and caught Sergeant MacGregor's eye.

MacGregor smiled vaguely.

'Well,' said Superintendent Underbarrow, struggling unobtrusively to retain what little contact he still had with the car seat, 'there it is. We'll never get that road passable until this rain stops.'

There were a few moments' silence, broken only by the hum of the police car's engine and the faint bubbling sound that was coming from Dover's lips.

Superintendent Underbarrow steeled himself to cast a mild aspersion. 'He's a bit of a rum one, isn't he?' he whispered.

MacGregor's smile became vaguer.

'I thought all the Yard's murder squad detectives were superintendents these days?'

'Well,' admitted MacGregor uneasily, 'strictly speaking they are.'

'But he's only a chief inspector.'

'That's right.'

'How come?'

'He's a sort of supernumerary,' MacGregor explained. The topic was a delicate one, though he might have been more forthcoming if he'd been certain that Dover was really asleep. 'He's just attached to the murder squad. Kind of seconded.'

'Oh.'· Superintendent Underbarrow looked unenlightened.

MacGregor groped around for a change of conversation. Chief Inspector Dover's somewhat chequered career was not a subject that a subordinate of even qualified loyalty would wish to have washed in public. One hardly cared to explain to a senior officer in another force that Dover was loosely attached to Scotland Yard's murder squad for the simple reason that nobody else in the length and breadth of the Metropolitan Police would have him.

MacGregor had just decided to make some pithy comment on the current economic crisis when the police car pulled into the side of the road and stopped.

'End of stage one,' grunted Superintendent Underbarrow as he opened his rear door. 'We've got to negotiate stage two by Land-Rover.'

'Really?'

'We had another bit of a landslide down here. Farming land, luckily, so there were no casualties, but the road's like Southend beach when the tide's out.' And on this somewhat cosmopolitan simile Superintendent Underbarrow extracted himself from the back seat and left it to MacGregor to rouse his master and explain the situation to him.

Dover was not pleased. He retaliated with a mixture of non-co-operation and bloody-mindedness so effectively that it took over ten minutes to carry out the transfer to the Land-Rover. Dover, as if of right, installed himself on the front seat next to the driver and left MacGregor and Superintendent Underbarrow to crouch miserably in the truck part at the back. The canvas roof leaked and they only had a couple of narrow wooden benches to sit on. With Dover's head already beginning to sink on to his breast, MacGregor had no choice but to carry on with the conversation.

He eased his kneecaps away from Superintendent Underbarrow's. 'You were talking about casualties, sir. There were several up at Sully Martin, weren't there?'

'Five dead and twenty injured,' agreed Superintendent Underbarrow proudly. 'Not bad for what the experts keep on insisting was a minor quake, is it? Mind you, they were only speaking seismographically.'

'And all these casualties were in the area of the cliff that broke away?'

Superintendent Underbarrow nodded. 'That's right. They reckon there was some sort of fault there and the earthquake just split it off. Freakish, really. One chunk of the village collapses and slithers off down the hill but, in the other part, you get nothing much worse than a few ornaments toppled off the mantelpiece.'

'So there was no damage in the rest of the village?'

'Not so's you'd notice.' Superintendent Underbarrow tried, unsuccessfully, to stretch his aching back. 'Well, the church steeple came down, of course, but you can't exactly count that. It was riddled with dry rot.'

'Really?'

'The vicar's been warning 'em for years, seemingly, but nobody was interested.'

'But I thought Sully Martin's church was part of our national heritage?'

'Oh, it is. A twelfth-century gem – scheduled and everything. But the steeple's much later. Mock Victorian Gothic, I think they call it. Anyhow, they're all as pleased as Punch it's gone.'

'Every cloud has a silver lining,' said MacGregor with a callous triteness he regretted as soon as the words were out.

Superintendent Underbarrow's mind, however, was more literal than sensitive. He bent double and glanced upwards through the windscreen. 'I wish those buggers up there'd show

13

theirs,' he grumbled. He gave the policeman driver a poke in the neck. 'Get your foot down, Rowney!' he admonished. 'We don't want to have to tackle that last bit in the dark.'

Rowney nodded, and the mud splashed up even higher from the wheels of the Land-Rover.

Superintendent Underbarrow settled back and regarded MacGregor glumly. 'That's why we didn't recognize it was murder,' he said abruptly.

'Sir?'

Superintendent Underbarrow sighed. He didn't hold with making excuses but his chief constable had been quite specific. The Scotland Yard men had to be told the whys and wherefores of the situation and made to realize that the local police were in no way to blame. It was the sort of cock-up that could have happened to anybody – given some rather exceptional circumstances.

The superintendent examined the polished toecaps of his shoes with great concentration. 'The earthquake happened just on two o'clock in the morning,' he began thoughtfully, 'so pretty well everybody was in bed. The whole thing only lasted ten or fifteen seconds so, by the time people had got up and thrown some clothes on, it was all over. The cliff had split off and a dozen or so houses and shops had gone down the hillside and were spread out all over the place. The main electric cables went and a couple of gas and water mains cracked open. Well, the villagers did what they could – rescuing people from the houses that were still tottering on the brink and all that sort of thing. Luckily the telephone wires were all right and they got a message through to us. We were on the scene in pretty quick time, all things considered, but we couldn't get any equipment up, of course. We did what we could but it wasn't until it was light, round about five, that we got the last of the wounded out of the mud and the debris and started on the corpses. I suppose it was well on into the afternoon before we'd got them all sorted out and identified and everything. That's when we first got a bit puzzled about Chantry.'

'Ah yes,' said MacGregor, taking considerably more interest now that this name had been mentioned.

'All the other dead and wounded had come from the houses that had collapsed and slipped down the cliff. They were all in their night clothes and we found them mostly still in bed, or still in their homes at any rate. Now, Chantry was in gum boots and a thick mackintosh and his house hadn't even been damaged. Well, we sort of jumped to the obvious conclusion.'

If MacGregor had a fault, it was that he tended to be too clever by half. He was finding Superintendent Underbarrow's recital rather tedious and he couldn't resist the temptation to try and speed things up a bit. 'You deduced that Mr Chantry had been engaged on the rescue operations, sir, and that he had somehow been killed accidentally?'

'That's about it, sergeant,' agreed the superintendent, quite without rancour. 'After the 'quake was over there were naturally several more landslips and odd bits of buildings kept falling down. Chantry still had his pyjamas on under his outer clothing and he was just the sort of chap who would have been first on the scene. It looked like a hero's death. That was before the doctor had a look at him, of course.'

'And then?'

'Manual strangulation.' Superintendent Underbarrow sighed. 'That put the cat amongst the pigeons, I can tell you.'

The Land-Rover stopped with a jerk and a skid. Dover came abruptly out of the Land of Nod and stared disconsolately about him.

The police driver turned round to report. 'Sorry, sir,' he said to Superintendent Underbarrow, 'but this is it. I can't get any farther.'

'Right!' The superintendent grinned at MacGregor and confirmed his worst fears. 'Come on, sergeant! It's shanks's pony now.'

'What?' Chief Inspector Dover came roaring back to full consciousness with both fists up.

'It's only just up the hill,' Superintendent Underbarrow

assured him genially. 'Shouldn't take us more than half an hour. What size shoes do you take?'

'Shoes?' Dover's piggy little eyes popped.

'You'll need gum boots and I'll try and borrow a couple of oilskins for you. Rowney, you'd better come up with us and help with the luggage.'

'Very good sir.' The police driver switched his engine off and got out of the Land-Rover.

Superintendent Underbarrow and MacGregor began to extract themselves from the rear but Dover sat firm.

'Just a minute,' he said.

Superintendent Underbarrow paused. 'Time's getting on,' he warned. 'It's no joke, getting up there in the dark.'

'Earthquakes,' said Dover. 'Suppose there's another one?'

Superintendent Underbarrow eyed him with mild dislike. This joker was a right specimen and no mistake. 'Not much chance of that,' he lied blandly. 'Like lightning, you know. Never strikes twice in the same place.'

Dover sniffed suspiciously. 'You sure?'

MacGregor opened his mouth but, at a glance from Superintendent Underbarrow, shut it again.

'Quite sure,' said Superintendent Underbarrow.

Eventually, gum-booted and festooned in oilskins, the little convoy set off up the hill. A group of council workmen, knocking off after another day's unrewarding struggle with the mud, cheered and whistled them on their way. Police Constable Rowney and Superintendent Underbarrow carried the luggage between them. The suitcases were heavy but they were as nothing compared to Dover. The task of getting him up to Sully Martin was dropped squarely on MacGregor's shoulders. The rain tippled down as they slipped and scrambled along. Here and there somebody had tried to improve the going by arranging chunks of masonry as stepping stones but the tide of mud was already engulfing them.

Dover, never an enthusiast for physical exertion in the choicest of circumstances, slithered and panted and blasphemed.

Before long he got one arm round MacGregor's neck and hung there with the grim tenacity of an obese and cowardly limpet. MacGregor's protests that he couldn't breathe fell on deaf ears.

'If we go, laddie,' promised Dover with a snarl, 'we go together!'

Onwards and upwards. At long last MacGregor hauled his chief inspector's seventeen and a quarter stone as far as a line of partially submerged duckboards where Superintendent Underbarrow, his good nature getting the better of him once again, was waiting for them with guidance and encouragement.

'Not much farther now!' he called.

'Bloody oaf!' muttered Dover into MacGregor's left ear. 'I'm warning you, laddie! Much more of him and there'll be another murder!'

The duckboarding was only a foot or so wide and further progress could only be achieved in single file. With some difficulty MacGregor managed to wean Dover from his stranglehold and get him to lead the way. Superintendent Underbarrow brought up the rear and, finding himself next to MacGregor, resumed their interrupted conversation.

'Aye,' he began, 'manual strangulation.'

MacGregor spoke back over his shoulder. 'The murderer must have been a bit of an idiot, sir.'

'How d'you mean?'

'Well, if he'd just battered Chantry's head in with a piece of wood or a brick, you'd probably be none the wiser, would you, sir? It would have just gone down in the book as an accident.'

'Hm.' Superintendent Underbarrow decided after a moment's reflection that it wasn't worth taking offence at this implied slur on his colleagues' efficiency. 'He probably never thought of that.'

'Killed in a moment of blind passion, you think, sir?'

'Well, it can't have been premeditated, can it? Nobody could have foreseen there was going to be an earthquake.'

17

'Bit of an opportunist, eh?'

'It looks like that to me. And damned lucky, too. Chantry's body was found over there somewhere.' The superintendent pointed through the sheeting rain and the encroaching twilight. 'Looks like the back of the moon, doesn't it? Chaos,' he observed sadly. 'Sheer, utter and undiluted chaos. If you lot rely on footprints and fingerprints and things like that, you're in for a pretty thin time.'

Dover had reach the end of the duckboards.

'Turn right, chief inspector!' called Superintendent Underbarrow. He poked MacGregor between the shoulder blades. 'See that, sergeant?'

'That heap of stones, sir?'

'The old Sally Gate – or what's left of it. Stood here for centuries and now it looks for all the world like a pile of hard core for a motorway. They're talking about rebuilding it, but I don't know.' He put a spurt on and overtook Dover. 'We're in West Street now,' he told him, 'and just along here is the line of the fault where this part of the cliff cracked. It runs right across the village. All the damage was on this side – see?'

Dover couldn't have cared less about the blasted damage. He was too busy staring in dismay at a couple of narrow planks that had been thrown across the gaping ravine in the road. 'Strewth, they weren't expecting him to . . .?

They were.

Dover was rapidly reaching the end of his not very lengthy tether. After a short and completely futile argument he simply closed his eyes and left it to MacGregor and Superintendent Underbarrow to guide his hesitant feet across. They'd got him just about midway when there was a dull, heavy rumble from behind them. Even MacGregor went white.

'What was that?' he asked apprehensively. He was down on his knees trying to force Dover's left foot in front of his right.

Superintendent Underbarrow hastened to reassure him. 'They're still knocking a few of the wrecked houses down. It's too dangerous to leave 'em standing. Pity, really. Sully Martin was quite a pretty little place before all this happened.'

They reached the end of West Street and turned right into Cherry Lane. Superintendent Underbarrow began stamping the great clods of mud off his feet. 'Soon be there now,' he informed them cheerfully. 'We're over the worst. We've had to come a bit of a long way round, of course, but another couple of minutes should see us in the Blenheim Towers. And not before time, eh?'

A kindly darkness masked the sneer on Dover's face and the superintendent looked around for something else to interest his guests.

'There's the church,' he said, indicating a noble mediaeval pile on his left. 'It's a blessing that's still standing. There'd have been some glum faces knocking around if that had gone. You'll see where the steeple fell when we get round the corner into East Street.'

Chief Inspector Dover stumped wearily on. For all he cared, you could take every mediaeval church and steeple in Christendom and stuff 'em. He'd more serious problems on his mind. His feet and his stomach, to name but two. Both, of course, were always with him but at the moment they were causing him even more anxiety than usual. His stomach had been rumbling menacingly for some time and what those bloody wellington boots were doing to his feet didn't bear thinking about. Everybody knew rubber drew your feet something cruel and the last thing Dover's feet needed was drawing.

MacGregor, too, had other preoccupations though his were of a less personal nature. 'What sort of man was this Chantry fellow?' he asked.

'Walter Chantry?' repeated Superintendent Underbarrow. 'Well, I didn't really know him, of course. Sat on the same committees with him once or twice but that's about all. Middle-aged. Widower. Lived here in Sully Martin with his married daughter and her husband.'

'A professional man?'

'A builder. In a very good way of business, too, by all

accounts. Tragic, really. He'd have made a packet out of this lot, wouldn't he?' Superintendent Underbarrow chuckled softly to himself. 'Ah, well, that's life! We turn left again here, sergeant. Yes, a builder he was. Had his offices and yard over at Kellet Sands. Look – that's where the steeple came down. Right across this road – see? It blocked it completely for several hours but they've cleared it away now, of course. By the way, sergeant, you'll see what this means from your point of view?'

'Er – not exactly, sir.'

'Well, for an hour or more after the actual earthquake, that devastated part of the village where Chantry's body was found was completely cut off. The main road up through the old Sally Gate was blocked by the landside. West Street, the one we just came along, was cut by that ravine thing and I can't see anybody scrambling across that in the dark, can you?'

MacGregor bit his lip and looked thoughtfully around. 'And this street, East Street, was blocked by the fallen steeple?'

'That's right. It narrows the field of suspects down a bit.'

'And there's no other way through?'

'I suppose you could get across this central square area, here, through the churchyard perhaps and over a few garden walls, but it'd be far from easy. There's spikes and barbed wire and broken glass all over the place. Some of our lads explored it as a possible route this morning but they said it was well nigh hopeless. Well, if a couple of fit young coppers can't do it in broad daylight . . . Oh, we turn right down this lane here.' He turned back to call encouragingly over his shoulder to the bulky and glowering figure that was falling farther and farther behind. 'We're all but there, chief inspector!'

Dover's reply was inaudible but short.

At the end of the lane they came to a fair-sized house which stood rather primly in its own neglected looking grounds. Wrought-iron gates hung crazily open, their rusty hinges showing that they had not been used for many years. PC Rowney, still carrying his two suitcases, led the way up the short circular drive which swept, rather meanly and weedily, up to the front door.

Dover, dimly sensing that food, warmth and shelter were at long last within sight, caught up with the others just as they were mounting the short flight of steps.

'Home at last!' beamed Superintendent Underbarrow as Dover stopped dead in his tracks and stared up at the peeling sign which hung above the front door. 'You'll not be sorry to get in out of this rain, eh?'

The habitual bad-tempered expression on Dover's face gradually gave way to a scowl of bleak fury. His eyesight not being what it used to be, he read the sign again before exploding with an oath that set even PC Rowney's ears tingling.

Superintendent Underbarrow blinked. 'What's the matter?'

'That's the matter, you great gibbering idiot!' howled Dover and pointed a fat, trembling finger at the sign.

MacGregor felt an iron hand of apprehension clutch his heart. He scurried back down the front steps to see what it was that had reduced his superior officer to a quivering jelly of wrath.

Oh, God!

The sign was blistered and faint but perfectly legible. There was no mistaking its dreadful message. 'THE BLENHEIM TOWERS PRIVATE HOTEL,' it read. 'Unlicensed.'

Two

It was a good quarter of an hour before Dover's boiling rage could be reduced to a more manageable simmering sulk. The handful of residents and guests, who had gathered to have a discreet peep at the exciting new arrivals, retreated in some disorder to their rooms, the more timid ones amongst them going so far as to hide their heads under the bedclothes. Really, the language! It was much worse than the time the Reverend Adalbert Brown's partner had failed to return his lead when their opponents (vulnerable) were on a little slam in spades, doubled and redoubled.

The brunt of the vituperation was borne, of course, by a bewildered Superintendent Underbarrow. Even Dover couldn't hold Sergeant MacGregor entirely responsible for this particular catastrophe, much as he would have liked to. The superintendent, once he had grasped that Dover was not being funny, had hastened to defend himself and the accommodation he had chosen.

He began, mistakenly perhaps, with an appeal to reason. 'But there's nowhere else, old chap,' he told an empurpled Dover. 'This is the only available place.'

'A temperance boarding house?' screamed Dover. 'This

bug-infested chicken coop?'

'We've just had an earthquake,' explained Superintendent Underbarrow with commendable patience. 'Every house in the village with spare rooms has taken in refugees. There isn't a vacant bed anywhere.'

Dover bared his National Health teeth in a snarl of sheer exasperation. 'What about the local boozer, dolt? You could have shifted a couple of your bloody refugees out of there, couldn't you?'

'Sully Martin only had one public house,' replied Superintendent Underbarrow calmly, 'and that went over the cliff in the earthquake. It stood just inside the Sally Gate.'

Dover's jaw dropped. 'Do you mean we can't even get a drink?' he asked hoarsely.

'I'm afraid not.'

Dover illustrated his ability to make a quick decision in an emergency. 'MacGregor,' he bawled, 'get the suitcases!'

'Sir?'

'You don't think I'm stopping here, do you?'

'But there's nowhere else, sir.'

'Not in Sully bloody Martin, maybe – but there are plenty of other places, aren't there? Where's the nearest town?'

Superintendent Underbarrow shrugged his shoulders. He was beginning to go off the human race. 'If you want to tramp up that hill through all that muck and mud every day, that's your affair.'

Dover's outburst of righteous indignation evaporated as it usually did when his personal comfort was threatened. He capitulated with characteristic grace and charm. 'You'll have to ship a few bottles of booze up,' he informed Superintendent Underbarrow. 'Half a dozen bottles of Scotch and a couple of crates of stout'll do for a start. I have to have the stout for my stomach. You can charge 'em up to incidental expenses.'

'I can't do that.'

'Why not? 'Strewth, if a blooming superintendent can't cook a few books, who can?'

23

'It's not that. It's the transport problem. Until we get that road clear we've got to manhandle all the supplies up by brute force. It's taking us all our time to bring the basic necessities in – bread, meat, milk for the babies. Damn it all, Dover, you can't expect me to let little children go hungry just so that you can knock back a bottle of wallop whenever you feel like it.'

'It's medicinal!' snapped Dover. 'Doctor's orders. Besides, kids these days are all too fat. Do 'em a world of good to go on short commons for a bit.'

Superintendent Underbarrow eyed Dover coldly. 'Well,' he said grudgingly, 'I'll see what I can do but I'm not promising anything, mind. And it's not being put down to any incidental expenses, either. You'll have to pay for it yourself.'

There was an embarrassing pause. Dover looked hopefully at MacGregor, but MacGregor was staring with grim determination at the ceiling. An impasse had been reached. Dover resolved it by collapsing sulkily on to a near-by chair and gloomily indicating that he was now ready to have his gum boots removed. With a sigh of relief that they weren't going to have another nasty scene about money MacGregor carefully hitched up the knees of his trousers and knelt down.

PC Rowney caught Superintendent Underbarrow's eye. 'I think it's about time we were going, sir.'

Superintendent Underbarrow nodded. The sooner the better as far as he was concerned. He had, however, one last duty to perform. A small, youngish man had been popping his head in and out of the door which led back to the service quarters of the hotel. At last his acute impatience was rewarded and he bounced athletically forward to be introduced.

'This,' said Superintendent Underbarrow, without much interest, 'is Mr Lickes, the proprietor of the Blenheim Towers. Detective Chief Inspector Dover and Detective Sergeant MacGregor.'

'Delighted!' gurgled Mr Lickes and pirouetted over to the suitcases. 'Quite delighted!' He flexed one bicep with evident

24

pride and then flexed the other. 'May I conduct you gentlemen to your rooms?'

'Not till I've had some afternoon tea,' said Dover as MacGregor finished tying his bootlaces and stood up.

Mr Lickes slowly straightened up from the knees-full-bend position he had struck preparatory to picking up the suitcases. 'Afternoon tea?' he said doubtfully. 'But we're serving supper in five minutes.'

Superintendent Underbarrow and PC Rowney took their leave while the going was good. Dover didn't even notice them depart, being too busy browbeating a somewhat less bouncy Mr Lickes.

'Yes, I know it's only six o'clock,' admitted Mr Lickes, nervously lacing his fingers across his chest and then trying to drag his hands apart, 'but most of our guests are rather elderly and they like to eat early. Late meals upset their digestions, so they say. Actually, I suspect the real reason is that they want to sit and watch television all night but it doesn't make much difference, does it? I am here to serve my clientele and, if they want their supper at six o'clock, mine not to reason why.'

'We're clientele, too,' objected Dover, appalled at the prospect of fourteen hungry hours till breakfast.

Mr Lickes was now pressing his clenched fists into the small of his back. 'Ah, but you're only temporaries, you see. It's our residents I'm talking about. The people who live here. They're our bread and butter,' he panted as he swung his right arm round and round like a windmill. 'You, I'm afraid, are just the jam.'

Dover turned, as he frequently did in moments of crisis, on MacGregor. 'Well, don't just stand there like Patience on a monument! Do something!'

MacGregor smiled tentatively at Mr Lickes. 'I'm afraid, sir, that, because of the peculiar nature of our business here, we're going to make rather a lot of trouble for you.'

Mr Lickes ground his shoulder blades together and smiled back. 'Oh, no, you're not,' he assured MacGregor pleasantly.

MacGregor tried again. 'We may have to ask you for meals at rather inconvenient times.'

'No harm in asking,' came the courteous reply.

'We are here on official and very important duties, sir.'

'Breakfast at nine,' said Mr Lickes, 'lunch at half past twelve and supper at six. Unconsumed meals will be placed on the hot plate and may be eaten in the dining-room at the guest's own convenience. It's all written out on the card pinned behind your bedroom door. If that's what you'd like to do now,' he added, genuflecting gently and rhythmically, 'I shall be only too happy to oblige. You can eat when you feel like it.'

'Strewth!' groaned Dover.

'We've having frozen cod fingers, tinned peas and chips to-night,' Mr Lickes went on happily. 'The menu is decided by the relief organization that sends the food up. Saves us an awful lot of worry, I can tell you, not having to work out the menus. Oh – and reconstituted Scotch broth to start with and sago pudding for afters. Awful, isn't it? Still, this is a crisis and we must all tighten our belts.' He took a deep breath and held it for fifteen, vein-throbbing seconds. 'Mind you,' he blurted out with a gasp, 'we lay on cocoa, hot toast and dripping in the lounge at nine o'clock so nobody need go hungry to bed. And now,' – he broke off to touch his toes three times in quick succession – 'it's time for supper.'

Under the astonished gaze of Dover and MacGregor, Mr Lickes leapt for the huge brass gong that stood in one corner of the hall and, seizing the leather-covered stick, began to thrash mercilessly away.

The response was well nigh instantaneous. Down the stairs in a genteel stampede came the Blenheim Towers guests: two men, a teenage girl and three old ladies. Sparing only a brief sideways glance, they swept inexorably into the dining-room.

Mr Lickes watched them pass and replaced his gong stick with a flourish. 'Like the zoo, isn't it?' he asked in a conspiratorial whisper before following his livelihood through the open doorway.

Dover slowly shook his head. 'We've been dumped in a loony-bin,' he moaned. 'Did you see that lot?'

MacGregor nodded and tried to look on the bright side. 'I don't think they were too bad, sir. Some of them were rather elderly, perhaps, but . . .'

'Elderly?' snorted Dover. 'A couple of 'em had *rigor mortis* setting in!'

'Well, shall we wait till they've finished, sir, and have our meal later?'

'Warmed-up fish fingers?' asked Dover incredulously. 'If your stomach can stand that, you're lucky! Mine blooming well can't.' He heaved himself to his feet. 'Come on! You can take the suitcases upstairs afterwards.'

Mr Lickes shot forward to welcome them as they entered the dining-room. 'You're over there, gentlemen,' he informed them and nodded to a vacant table on which the white cloth was already heaving inauspiciously in the breeze. 'But, first, you must meet your fellow guests. We're all one big family here.'

It was a civility with which Dover would have been happy to dispense but Mr Lickes was not to be denied. He took hold of the chief inspector by the coat sleeve and led him over to the three old ladies. They were at the far end of the room but Mr Lickes was too wily a hotelier to ignore the demands of age, seniority of residence and sex.

Dover glowered with impartial dislike at Mrs Boyle, Miss Kettering and Miss Dewar. Their reactions, however, varied considerably. Mrs Boyle, the relict of a rear-admiral and a noted stickler for the ship-shape, stared in blank astonishment at the untidy hulk which confronted her.

'Interestin',' she remarked in a very loud voice to her companions. 'First time I've ever come across a peeler in good society. They'll be presentin' omnibus drivers to us next.'

It was not an observation calculated to endear her to Dover and he tied a mental knot in his mind to pin the murder on Mrs Boyle, if it was humanly possible.

Meanwhile Miss Dewar appeared to be trying to submerge

her scarlet face in her soup bowl. This was not the consequence of Mrs Boyle's somewhat unkind comments but Miss Dewar's normal reaction to any member of the male sex who came within twenty feet. She was, as she frequently told her female friends, a martyr to shyness.

Miss Kettering, on the other hand, wasn't. At sixty-two and with several very near misses behind her, she had not yet abandoned hope. MacGregor looked much the more enticing proposition, of course, but Miss Kettering was a realist and knew her limitations. She fixed her sights on Dover and ogled him relentlessly until Mr Lickes led him away to the next table.

Old Mr Revel was sitting alone. The batteries in his hearing-aid had run down and he hadn't the faintest idea who Dover and MacGregor were or what they were doing there. Nevertheless he greeted them like long-lost brothers and, staggering to his feet, would have enfolded them in a warm embrace if Dover hadn't fended him off with a well-directed shove in the chest. Mr Revel fell back, spluttering but not speechless.

'God bless you!' he quavered. 'I knew it would happen one day.' He flung a defiant, if watery, glance round the room. 'We've got the bitches outnumbered at last!'

Mr Lickes hurried Dover on. 'Bit of a misogynist, our Mr Revel,' he murmured. 'Always going on about being incarcerated in a matriarchal society. And now,' he said in a normal voice as he stopped at the third and last table, 'let me introduce you to our two earthquake victims. Their house was destroyed, you know, and they're staying with us until they can arrange other accommodation.'

Dover's stomach was now rumbling louder than ever and it was a lack-lustre eye that he turned on Wing Commander Bertram Pile (Retired) and his seventeen-year-old daughter, Linda. The indifference was mutual.

Mr Lickes conducted the two policemen over to their own table and improved the brief moment with a quiet warning. 'I should give those two a wide berth, if I were you,' he whispered. 'The girl's not quite all there – mentally retarded, you know – and her father tends to be a mite over-possessive. They keep themselves very much to themselves.'

Supper at the Blenheim Towers was consumed in total silence and at an incredible speed. Mr Lickes, who did the serving, flashed round the dining-room like a dancing dervish but even he had his work cut out. The trouble was, though, that while the diners had the table manners of ravenous wolves they hadn't got the appetites to match.

Dover, unsustained by a couple of mouthfuls of thin soup, regarded his fish fingers glumly. 'It's not enough to keep a bloody sparrow going!' he whined.

MacGregor tended to go off his food when he ate at the same table as Dover and so the sacrifice he was clearly being expected to make was not too severe.

Dover accepted the proffered plate and shovelled the contents on to his own. 'It still doesn't add up to more than half a proper helping,' he grumbled as he grabbed his knife and fork. 'Isn't there any tomato ketchup knocking around?' He removed a tiny fishbone from the back of his upper plate and dropped it fastidiously on the floor. ''Strewth, we'd be better off in one of those prisoner-of-war camps. First thing tomorrow morning you get on to that Wheelbarrow chap and tell him we want some parcels sending up.'

MacGregor made the mistake of smiling. 'Yes, sir.'

A mouthful of ginger-coloured breadcrumbs, which Dover could ill afford to lose, came spattering across the table. 'I'm not joking, you bloody fool!'

'No, sir!' MacGregor, knowing only too well the unpleasantnesses that could result from rubbing Dover up the wrong way, hastened to offer the only olive branch that lay to hand. 'I never eat sago pudding, sir. If you'd care to have mine . . .'

Coffee was served in the lounge but only half the Blenheim Towers contingent repaired there to consume it. Wing Commander Pile and his daughter hurried off immediately to their rooms and were followed at a slightly more dignified gait by Mrs Boyle and the still-blushing Miss Dewar. Dover, who had an eye for these things, beat the rest of the field to the most comfortable chair while MacGregor politely undertook to pour out the coffee. Old Mr Revel shuffled off into a dark corner and switched on the television set. Miss Kettering tiptoed elaborately after him and turned the volume control right down.

'He can't hear a thing,' she confided in Dover as she joined him by the fire with a coy giggle, 'and he's perfectly happy just watching the pictures.'

There was an unencouraging grunt from Dover but, good heavens, if Miss Kettering allowed herself to be put off by little things like that, she'd never make friends with *anybody*!

'I think we watch too much television these days, don't you?' she pressed on. 'Everybody says it's ruining the art of conversation.'

Dover snorted unpleasantly and rudely down his nose.

Miss Kettering responded with a merry laugh. 'You've got a bit of a cold coming on, haven't you?'

'More than likely,' said Dover, brightening up a bit.

'Bed,' said Miss Kettering firmly.

'Eh?'

'Two aspirins, a hot whisky and stay in bed until you feel better – it's the only treatment.'

Dover began to regard Miss Kettering in a more favourable light. He was second to none in appreciating people who took a sympathetic interest in his health. 'There's only one snag,' he said, trying to talk down his nose. 'No whisky.'

Miss Kettering glanced round to make sure that they could not be overheard. 'Mrs Boyle has a small bottle in her handbag,' she whispered. 'Purely medicinal – so she says.'

'Perhaps she'd lend me a drop?' Dover whispered hopefully back.

'Not if you were dying in front of her, dear! She's terribly mean. Oh,' – Miss Kettering jumped a little as MacGregor bowed in front of her with three cups of coffee on a tray – 'how very kind!'

When Miss Kettering had refused sugar and Dover had dug

out his six spoonfuls, MacGregor sat down too. Unlike some people he could name, he never forgot that he was a detective or that he was supposed to be on duty. After one refreshing sip of his coffee, he got down to business.

'Were you here when the earthquake happened, Miss Kettering?' he asked as though merely making polite conversation.

Dover rolled his eyes and sank back resentfully in his chair as the flood gates burst open.

Miss Kettering certainly was here when the earthquake happened and she couldn't begin to tell them what a horrifying experience it had been. She would remember that dreadful night until her dying day, and probably after it. 'Of course,' – she was perched on the edge of her chair, transported by the joy of addressing a masculine and (as far as earthquakes were concerned) virgin audience – 'it came completely without warning, you see. That's what made it such a terrible shock. If only they'd told us on the weather forecast . . .'

'Were you in bed?' asked MacGregor.

Miss Kettering's heart fluttered. That was twice already that bed had reared its fascinating head in the conversation! 'Yes, I was,' she admitted daringly. 'It was the middle of the night, you know. Of course, I simply leapt out when I felt everything rocking and shaking. The awful part was not knowing what it was. My first thought was that those dreadful Chinese had struck at last. There wasn't as much noise as I would have expected but they're supposed to be frightfully cunning, aren't they? I'm sure a silent atomic bomb wouldn't be beyond their fiendish minds.'

MacGregor avoided catching Dover's jaundiced eye and concentrated on steering Miss Kettering back on more profitable rails. 'What did you do after you'd jumped out of bed, madam?'

'Well, I grabbed my crystal ball, as a matter of fact,' said Miss Kettering with a deprecating laugh. 'I wasn't going to let that get broken if I could possibly help it. It's such a comfort to me, you know, and they're terribly expensive things to replace. I wrapped it up in my best bed-jacket and rushed off to see if Miss Dewar was all right.'

'And was she?'

'Oh, yes – apart from being scared out of what few wits she still possesses. She'd got up, too, and gone into Mrs Boyle's room. In the end all three of us spent the rest of the night there. Miss Dewar and I curled up as best we could on a couple of chairs while Mrs Boyle just stayed in bed, looking" – a rather malicious gleam appeared in Miss Kettering's eye – 'like the Rock of Gibraltar. Such a source of strength to the rest of us! She knew it was an earthquake, of course, having been connected with the navy for so long. She's always right about things like that. She doesn't believe in standing for any nonsense either, you know. She was quite sharp when poor Miss Dewar kept snivelling that it was the end of the world and I had to be frightfully careful that she didn't spot my poor old crystal ball. When I realized that there was no danger of contamination by fall-out, I suggested we might be safer outside in the open air but Mrs Boyle wasn't having any of that either. Mind you, it was raining very heavily.'

'I see,' said MacGregor, digesting these snippets of information carefully. 'So you, Mrs Boyle and Miss Dewar remained here in the hotel and in each other's company for the remainder of that night?'

'Yes.' Miss Kettering regarded MacGregor shrewdly. 'So we couldn't have murdered Mr Chantry, could we?'

'Has anybody suggested that you did, madam?'

'Not so far but, presumably, everybody in the village is more or less under suspicion. What time was Mr Chantry actually killed?'

MacGregor, in spite of his elegant appearance, was a real policeman. He preferred asking questions to answering them. 'Oh, some time before dawn,' he said reluctantly.

'Well, I can vouch for Mrs Boyle and Miss Dewar until after lunch when we all went to our rooms for a rest, and they'll be able to vouch for me. We were never out of each other's sight for more than a couple of minutes. I was all for going to help with the rescue work but Mrs Boyle said I'd be more trouble than I was worth, and she was probably right. Still, I felt guilty about just sitting here.'

Dover bestirred himself. He gave a tremendous yawn and scratched his head. The dandruff fell in a shower on his shoulders. 'Anybody got a fag?' he asked.

When he had got Dover contentedly dribbling ash down the lapels of his jacket, MacGregor resumed his interrogation. 'What about the other people in the hotel?'

'The other people?' Miss Kettering hesitated. She didn't exactly relish the role of police informer but, on the other hand, she couldn't see what harm it would do. Whoever had murdered Mr Chantry, it wasn't anybody from the Blenheim Towers, of that she was quite sure. 'Well, there weren't all that many other people here, actually. Only Mr Revel. Wing Commander Pile and Linda didn't join us until after the earthquake, of course.'

MacGregor glanced across at Mr Revel, who was still absorbed in the silent flickerings of his television screen. 'Did he leave the hotel?'

'Mr Revel?' Miss Kettering's mouth dropped open but then she recovered her sense of humour and gave MacGregor a reproving slap on the knee. 'Silly boy!'

'We have to check on everybody, madam,' MacGregor pointed out stiffly.

'But you might as well suspect me, dear!'

MacGregor studiously said nothing.

Miss Kettering sighed. She had thought that hob-nobbing with a couple of real live Scotland Yard detectives was going to be such *fun*. 'To the best of my knowledge,' she said distantly, 'Mr Revel has not left the grounds of this hotel for the last five years. Even on one of his good days it takes him at least two hours to get to the gates at the bottom of the drive. If you think he is capable of making his way as far as North Street in the pitch dark and murdering a man forty years his junior with his bare hands – well,' – Miss Kettering paused for breath and grammatical orientation – 'you must have a very vivid imagination, that's all I can say. Leave the hotel? Why, the poor old thing didn't even wake up. He slept right through till breakfast time like a babe in arms.'

'You're sure of that?'

'Of course I'm sure of it. At breakfast time Mrs Boyle and Miss Dewar and I spent twenty minutes trying to explain things to him. Even when he understood us, he wouldn't believe us. It's a point of principle with him not to believe anything any woman tells him. We just had to wait until Mr Lickes had time to cope with him.'

'Ah, Mr Lickes!' MacGregor restrained himself from pouncing too ferociously. 'I suppose he left the hotel, did he?'

'What would you expect him to do?' demanded Miss Kettering tartly. 'Cower under the beds like the rest of the silly old women in this place? We could hear all those people screaming and shouting quite distinctly, you know. It was obvious that something terrible had happened. Both Mr and Mrs Lickes rushed out to help as soon as they'd pulled some clothes on and been round to see that the rest of us were all right. Mrs Lickes came back after a bit to make tea and sandwiches for the rescue workers and the injured but Mr Lickes didn't return until much later. He was nearly dead on his feet, poor man. He . . .'

Dover perked up again, revived by the mention of food and drink. 'What time do they bring this toast stuff round?'

'Oh, not for ages yet, dear.' Miss Kettering came to a painful decision. Masculine company or no masculine company, she had had enough of being grilled for one evening. She eyed MacGregor severely. Maybe she was growing old but, really, she did find the young so *brutal* these days! She stood up.

'You going?' The question came from Dover who, while not exactly enamoured of Miss Kettering, had no wish to be left *tête-à-tête* with his sergeant.

Miss Kettering smiled down at him. At least he hadn't treated her like a potential murderess. 'I really think I ought to go and do a little more work on my correspondence course. What with all the upheavals of the last day or so, I've been rather neglecting it.'

MacGregor, whose manners were really beyond reproach, got to his feet. He realized that he had upset Miss Kettering and he tried to make amends. 'A correspondence course, Miss Kettering?' he inquired pleasantly. 'What is it you're studying?'

'Witchcraft,' said Miss Kettering and, knowing she couldn't better that, made her exit with dignity and style.

MacGregor shrugged his shoulders. You met all sorts in his profession. He sat down again and pulled out his notebook.

Dover's face relaxed back into a peevish scowl. Couldn't the blasted young whipper-snapper think about anything else but work? 'What are you doing?' he growled.

'Just making a few notes, sir.'

'I can see that, idiot! What about?'

With great forbearance MacGregor closed his notebook and prepared to explain the situation as simply as possible. 'All the inhabitants of this hotel, sir, are suspects.'

'This collection of old rag-bags? You must be potty!'

'I agree that most of them don't look very likely, sir, but – unlike the greater part of the village – they did have the opportunity.'

'Wadderyermean – unlike the greater part of the village? I thought everybody in this dump from the cat upwards was a starter.'

MacGregor smiled rather smugly. 'I'm afraid you must have missed what Superintendent Underbarrow was telling us, sir. You see, Chantry's body was found in what we might call the disaster area proper – where the cliff broke away and the houses were destroyed. It seems reasonable to suppose that he was killed there, too. Well, now,' – MacGregor leaned forward as he got into his stride – 'assuming that the murder took place after the earthquake, the number of people who could have reached the scene of the crime is strictly limited.'

'Why?'

'The only means of access were blocked, sir. West Street had that great crevice across it, the one we came over, and East Street was barred by the collapse of the church steeple. That means that most people in the village couldn't get to the disaster area for some considerable time. By when, of course, Chantry was dead. We can rule out any outsider being involved because, as you know, the main road was blocked, too. On the face of it, it looks as though the murderer must have come from this part of the village. That is, sir, from the area nearest to the disaster area and on this side of the two obstacles cutting off . . .'

'Sounds a bit thin to me,' said Dover sourly.

'Well, we shall have to check, sir, but it looks a reasonable working hypothesis, I think.'

Dover lapsed into a moody contemplation of the fire. This investigation had got the mockers on it from the start, any moron could see that. He wondered morosely how soon he could decently chuck his hand in and get back to civilization and all the comforts of home. A couple of days? No, p'raps he'd better stretch it out a bit longer than that, otherwise they'd be dropping on him like a ton of bricks and accusing him of not trying again. Nobody knew better than Dover the importance of choosing the psychological moment for conceding defeat.

'Of course, sir,' – MacGregor had opened his notebook again – 'I'm not really considering Mr Revel and the three old ladies very seriously, but Mr Lickes is a different proposition. There's his wife too.'

Dover cleared his throat and MacGregor waited respectfully for the oracle to speak. 'You taken the suitcases upstairs yet, laddie?'

'No, sir. Should I do it now?'

'Might as well,' said Dover through another enormous yawn.

'I think I'll come up with you and have an early night.'

'You're not going to wait for the cocoa and toast, sir?'

'No.' Dover dragged himself laboriously to his feet. 'You can fetch it up to me and I'll have it in bed.'

Three

'What in the name of heaven's going on here?'

Mr Lickes removed his eye from the keyhole in the dining-room door and looked up to see who it was standing in the hall. 'Oh, Superintendent Underbarrow? Am I glad to see you!'

'What's happening?' Superintendent Underbarrow closed the front door behind him and removed his cap. 'You can hear the shouting right down at the drive gates.'

'I think you may just be in time to prevent a lynching,' – Mr Lickes bent down to his keyhole again – 'if you hurry.'

'A lynching?' Superintendent Underbarrow regarded the prospect with equanimity. Well, you didn't have lynchings in places like the Blenheim Towers Private Hotel, not at nine o'clock in the morning, you didn't. 'Who's going to be lynched?'

Mr Lickes straightened up with a sigh. 'That young police sergeant you brought up last night. It's not his fault, of course, but Mrs Boyle is out for blood and she's got past caring whose blood it is.' He gestured helplessly at the dining-room door. 'She's flashing her table knife around in there in a very alarming manner. I'm afraid I cleared out when I saw things beginning to get nasty. Otherwise they'd have turned on me.'

'Discretion is the better part of valour,' observed Superintendent Underbarrow.

Mr Lickes performed a couple of half-hearted kicks. 'Aren't you going in there and break it up?'

'In my experience some passions are actually inflamed by the sight of a police uniform. It's all a question of timing.'

Mr Lickes nodded understandingly. 'I dare say that young fellow knows how to look after himself. Well,' – he indicated a couple of chairs – 'we might as well make ourselves comfortable while we're waiting.'

They sat down and listened for a few minutes to the uproar which was still coming unabated from the dining-room.

'You still haven't told me what's up,' said Superintendent Underbarrow.

Mr Lickes desisted from his efforts to lift himself and his chair off the ground. 'I suppose it really started last night – when they saw their rooms.'

'It's Chief Inspector Dover and Sergeant MacGregor we're talking about, is it?'

Mr Lickes nodded. 'I knew that fat one was going to be a trouble-maker as soon as I saw him. You develop a sort of instinct.'

'What did he do?'

'Played merry hell when he found they were up on the top floor. You should have heard him! Well, I know those rooms are only converted attics but they're none the worse for that. Besides, where else could I put him? All the rooms on the first floor are full.'

'I did wonder about those stairs,' mused Superintendent Underbarrow. 'They're none too well lit.'

'They're perfectly safe, if you're careful.'

'Steep, though,' said Superintendent Underbarrow, 'and narrow. Even I found 'em a bit awkward and I'm a jolly sight nippier than he is.'

'It's those two rooms on the second floor or a tent out on the lawn. I told him that.'

'He's a big man,' Superintendent Underbarrow went on. 'Clumsy. One slip and he'd break his bloody neck. I didn't think he'd relish those stairs.'

Mr Lickes pushed his left fist desperately against the palm of his right hand. 'It wasn't only the stairs.'

'No?'

'Well, the stairs and the bathroom, really.'

'Go on!'

'The bathroom's on the first floor.'

'Ah!'

'It was pure spite. I'm sure of that.'

'Really?'

'Five times last night.'

'Never!'

'And he woke the whole house up every time. Clumping up and down those stairs with his boots on, slamming doors, flushing the cistern as though it was Niagara Falls. Nobody got a wink of sleep all night.'

Superintendent Underbarrow glanced thoughtfully at the dining-room door. 'So that's what they're kicking up their fuss about?'

'You can hardly blame them, can you? Mrs Boyle's a martyr to insomnia at the best of times. I knew we'd be in for the mother and father of all rows this morning.'

Superintendent Underbarrow tried to be helpful. 'Maybe if you had a quiet word with him?'

The dining-room door burst open before Mr Lickes had time to reply and a dishevelled looking MacGregor came hurtling out. He was balancing a loaded breakfast tray in his hands.

'Morning, sergeant!' said Superintendent Underbarrow, relieved that things seemed to be working themselves out without his assistance.

MacGregor all but dropped his tray. 'Oh, good morning,

sir!' He turned back and closed the dining-room door. 'I wasn't expecting to see you this morning, sir.'

'I thought I'd just pop in and take you on a conducted tour of the battlefield – you know – where the body was found. You've got all the photographs and plans, of course, but it's a bit of a job deciding what's what, even so.'

'That's extremely kind of you, sir.' MacGregor glanced down in some embarrassment at the tray in his hands. 'I'm not sure whether Chief Inspector Dover will be able to make it. As a matter of fact, he's still – er – in bed.'

Superintendent Underbarrow kept his voice nicely neutral. 'Is he?'

'He's not feeling very well,' explained MacGregor, looking as awkward as he felt.

'I hope it's nothing serious.'

'He thinks he may have caught a bit of a chill. Anyhow,' – MacGregor took a firmer grip on his tray – 'I'll just run upstairs, sir, and see what he says.'

What Dover said, as he stretched out both hands to grab the tray, was regrettably predictable. ''Strewth, you've taken your bleeding time, haven't you? I could die of starvation up here for all you care.'

MacGregor struggled to get his breath back and decided that it was no time to regale Dover with even a tactful account of the protest meeting in the dining-room. 'Superintendent Underbarrow is downstairs, sir.'

The response arrived mixed with Rice Crispies. 'Well, you bloody well see he stops there!'

'He was going to show us where Chantry was found, sir.'

Dover pushed the remaining Rice Crispies on to his spoon with his finger. 'Who's Chantry?'

One day, MacGregor promised himself grimly, I'll split the stinking old bastard's skull wide open for him. 'Walter Chantry is the man who was murdered, sir.'

Dover, well into his bacon and eggs, wasn't interested. 'Old

Wheelbarrow can show you the sights,' he decided. 'Just keep him out of my hair, that's all.'

'You're going to stay in bed all day, sir?'

'You've got to look after a cold,' retorted Dover peevishly, 'or it might turn into something serious. I should have thought even a fool like you would have known that.'

MacGregor began to edge towards the door. 'Well, I'll just carry on alone until you're feeling better, shall I, sir?'

Dover paused in mid-mastication as all the warning bells began ringing. Give this toffee-nosed pup an inch and he finished up solving your blooming case for you! Dover had had trouble with this sort of thing in the past. He didn't give a monkey's whether the Sully Martin murderer was ever brought to book or not, but he was blowed if he was going to sit idly by while MacGregor sneaked in and garnered all the kudos. 'Hold it!' he rumbled.

MacGregor removed his hand from the door knob.

'Don't you go questioning anybody!'

MacGregor's face fell. 'But, sir . . .'

'But nothing! I'll do the interviewing, so you keep your greedy paws off!'

MacGregor tried to argue. In all police investigations, particularly murder ones, speed was essential. This was an elementary point which Dover had not yet grasped and it seemed unlikely now that he ever would.

'Poppycock!' he scoffed, covering his toast and most of the eiderdown with marmalade. 'Make haste slowly, that's my motto. And don't start yapping about preserving clues and all that textbook tripe you've picked up! In this case there aren't any bloody clues left. They wouldn't have called us in if there had been. And now, push off! I don't want to see your ugly mug again till you bring my lunch up at one o'clock sharp.'

'Have you any message for Superintendent Underbarrow, sir?' asked MacGregor, the prospect of a morning free from Dover's company making him careless.

Dover had – but it was not one which a sergeant could very

42

well pass on to a superintendent, however good natured.

MacGregor collected his oilskins and gum boots from his room and was half-way downstairs when he realized that the indignation meeting had moved from the dining-room to the entrance hall. Tactfully he withdrew into the shadows.

Mrs Boyle was still in good voice. 'What's wrong with givin' the brute a chamber pot?' she boomed at a cringing Mr Lickes. 'Seems to me an admirable solution.'

Mr Lickes mumbled something.

'I have a spare one in my leather trunk,' thundered Mrs Boyle. 'Don't usually make a habit of lendin' my personal possessions but, in this case, I'm prepared to make an exception. Tell your wife to come along and collect it later this mornin'.'

Mr Lickes's dry lips trembled again.

Mrs Boyle drew herself up. Indignation was written in every generous curve. 'Well, I hope you're not suggestin' that I should empty it, Lickes?'

Mr Lickes weakly shook his head.

'I'm glad to hear it.' Mrs Boyle regarded Mr Lickes severely. 'If you and your wife are, as usual, too overworked to perform your proper duties, I can only propose that the emptyin' of the utensil is entrusted to the brute's manservant.'

Mr Lickes apparently whispered yet another objection but Mrs Boyle was already leading the way to the lounge.

She tossed her final remarks back over her shoulder. 'I fail to see that the young man bein' a policeman makes any difference. It is doubtless like the army. Officers' batmen are themselves soldiers, are they not?'

Only when the Blenheim Towers guests had all dutifully followed Mrs Boyle and the lounge door was closed did MacGregor venture out of hiding. Mr Lickes saw him coming and fled to the sanctuary of the kitchen quarters.

'Ready are you, sergeant?' asked Superintendent Underbarrow, kindly refraining from comment.

MacGregor nodded his head.

'Bit of a mess, isn't it?' Superintendent Underbarrow examined the scene of devastation which spread before and below them with a certain amount of gloomy satisfaction. 'Worse than you expected, I'll bet.'

'Much worse, sir,' agreed MacGregor, taking a step or two back from the slimy edge of the cliff and unfolding his map. 'And there was a complete row of houses here?'

Superintendent Underbarrow pointed over to his left. 'That's where the Sally Gate was, remember? Then there was a pub, a couple of shops, four cottages and Wing Commander Pile's house here on the corner of what used to be Sidle Alley.'

'Sidle Alley?' queried MacGregor, looking at his map again. 'Oh, I see. It ran round the back there and down to the main road?'

'That's right. Luckily it was mostly barns and sheds and garages along there so we didn't have any casualties. And then,' – he gesticulated over to his right – 'the damage gets progressively less as you get beyond Sidle Alley. Starting with Wing Commander Pile's house here, the houses were only partially destroyed by the earthquake. The fronts, facing us, were still standing the morning after but, of course, they were in a very dangerous condition and the heavy rescue people had to knock them down. The people who lived in 'em made one hell of a fuss but there was nothing else you could do.'

'And whereabouts was Chantry's body found, sir?'

Superintendent Underbarrow led the way over towards the Sally Gate and, stepping over a make-shift rope barrier, stood on the very edge of the drop. 'Well, down there somewhere.'

MacGregor sighed. 'That doesn't look very helpful, sir.'

'No. He could have been killed up here somewhere and just slipped down with all the rest of the debris, or he could have been chucked over the edge after he was dead by the murderer. I doubt if there's any way of telling now.'

MacGregor watched a group of workmen who were busy trying to shore up the crumbling lip of the cliff to prevent further landslides. 'The other people who were killed, sir, – were they in this part, too?'

'All except one. They came from the pub and the two shops next door to it. Mind you, they were found in the ruins of their houses. Chantry's body, of course, was more or less on top.'

'That certainly makes it look as though he was killed after the earthquake,' said MacGregor, folding up his map and putting it away in his pocket.

Superintendent Underbarrow looked surprised. 'There's no doubt about that, is there?'

'We can't afford to overlook any possibility, sir.'

'But Chantry was out helping with the rescue work,' objected Superintendent Underbarrow as he began to move away to the undamaged side of North Street. 'Several people saw him.'

MacGregor picked his way carefully round a pile of planks and red warning lamps. 'I've been thinking about that, sir. Now, say I killed Chantry before the earthquake and just left him lying around in a corner somewhere. Then the earthquake happens and I seize the opportunity to confuse the issue. It was pitch dark and everybody must have been very upset and bewildered. All I have to do is point out some distant figure and refer to him as Chantry. Next morning, with a bit of luck, there may be several people who think quite seriously that they really had seen Chantry.'

'Well, it's an idea,' admitted Superintendent Underbarrow unwillingly, 'but there's his daughter's evidence, too. She said quite definitely that Chantry didn't leave the house until after the earthquake.'

MacGregor had an answer for that. 'She may be mistaken – or lying.'

'Lying? Why should she?'

MacGregor shrugged his shoulders. 'She may have killed her father.'

'That sounds a bit far-fetched.'

'She wouldn't be the first, sir. On the other hand, she may be protecting her husband.' MacGregor changed the conversation. Superintendent Underbarrow was a very decent chap but he wasn't CID. These uniformed fellows didn't really understand the problems. 'Where is Chantry's house, by the way?'

'Just here.' Superintendent Underbarrow nodded at a large well-cared-for residence, standing on the corner of North Street and East Street. 'Practically undamaged, as you can see.'

MacGregor looked around. 'And practically opposite Wing Commander Pile's house.'

'That's right.'

'Interesting,' commented MacGregor in an unworthy attempt to mystify the superintendent. 'Now, sir, I wonder if you could let me have a list of all the people who were involved in any way in this incident?'

'You mean the people who weren't cut off by the broken road in West Street and the church steeple? Yes,' – Superintendent Underbarrow began to fumble in his pocket – 'I think we can provide you with that all right.' He produced several sheets of paper covered with typewritten lists. 'This is a complete census of the village that was taken immediately after the earthquake. Now all we've got to do is check the addresses.' He fumbled about again and brought out a ball-point pen. 'I'll tick off the ones that could have been involved.'

By the time MacGregor got back to the Blenheim Towers just before one o'clock he was really feeling quite chirpy. That's what a morning away from Dover did for you! Still – apart from that – MacGregor considered himself entitled to some self-congratulation. All in all, he had made considerable progress. He had inspected the epicentre of Sully Martin's earthquake and seen the site, for what it was worth, of where Chantry's body was found and got a list of all the people upon whom suspicion might possibly fall. A good morning's work!

Now all he had to do was ensure that a certain person didn't frustrate all further developments.

Dover was ready and waiting for his lunch. MacGregor, showing a lamentable amount of low cunning, had procured a jumbo-sized helping of steak and kidney pudding for him. If that didn't send the old fool off to sleep for the rest of the afternoon, nothing would!

Dover demanded a detailed account of the morning's activities. ''Strewth,' he commented, 'you've not exactly been straining yourself, have you?' MacGregor, still hoping against hope for a free rein, sought for the soft answer but, before he'd found it, Dover was grousing on. 'The trouble with you, laddie, is you do damn-all if you haven't got somebody standing over you all the time. Now, let's have a look at this list of suspects.'

The reluctance with which MacGregor took the sheets of paper out of his pocket was not lost upon Dover. The chief inspector may have had his shortcomings but allowing himself to be upstaged by a snotty-nosed sergeant was not one of them. He ran a practised, if jaundiced, eye over the names and addresses.

'I thought I should perhaps make a start on seeing some of these people this afternoon, sir,' ventured MacGregor.

'Good idea,' murmured Dover. 'Strike while the scent's still warm, eh?'

'If you've finished the marmalade pudding, sir, there's some cheese and biscuits to follow.' MacGregor got up with pathetic eagerness to change the plates over.

Dover reclined back amiably on his pillows. 'Got your notebook handy, laddie?'

'Yes, sir.'

'Good. Well now, I reckon we'd better split this lot between us. We'll do a preliminary investigation so's we can weed out the sheep from the goats.'

MacGregor's hopes began to wane. 'Yes, sir.'

Dover grinned. It was like taking sweets off a baby, and just as enjoyable. 'Right! Well, I'll take Chantry's daughter and her husband, Wing Commander Pile and his daughter – you writing all this down, laddie? – and Mr and Mrs Lickes. You can do the rest.'

MacGregor's shoulders sagged. God knows how the old fool had done it, but he had skimmed the cream off that list with an unerring hand. All that MacGregor had been left with was an uninspiring collection of old age pensioners and gormless villagers whose murderous inclinations had long since been dissipated in other, more enjoyable, rural pursuits. He poured out Dover's coffee, picked the sheets of paper up off the floor and played his last card. 'Do you think it's wise, sir?'

'Probably not,' said Dover, 'but I can't do it all single-handed, can I?'

MacGregor gritted his teeth. 'I really meant with your cold, sir.'

'What about my cold?'

'Well, the weather's rotten outside, sir, really chilly and damp. And, of course, the village is ankle-deep in mud, as you already know. I was just wondering if it was really such a good idea for you to go out this afternoon when you've got such a bad cold.'

'Who said I was going out this afternoon?' demanded Dover.

'Oh, sir, I honestly don't think we ought to put these interviews off any longer. There's been enough delay on this case as it is and . . .'

'I shall conduct the interviews here,' said Dover, snapping his fingers imperiously for a cigarette. 'You don't want me to catch my blooming death, do you?'

MacGregor reached for his cigarette case and refrained from answering what was no doubt a rhetorical question. 'Oh, I hadn't thought of that, sir. Of course it will be much better for you to stay in the hotel and keep . . .'

'Not only in the hotel, laddie! I'm staying here, in bed. And now, if you've finished lolling around on your backside, you can buzz off and get things organized. I'll see Lickes in ten minutes and then his wife after him. Tell Pile and his potty daughter to stick around because I'll do them after the Lickeses.'

'And Mr and Mrs Hooper, sir? That's Chantry's daughter and her . . .'

'I know who Mr and Mrs Hooper are!' roared Dover. 'I'll see them later on. You can call round on your way out and tell 'em I want 'em around here at seven tonight.'

'Very well, sir.' McGregor rose to his feet. 'I'll send Mr Lickes up in ten minutes, shall I?'

'If it's not too much trouble,' said Dover with heavy sarcasm. 'Here – take the blooming tray down with you, moron!'

Mr Lickes had been born and brought up in the hotel business and so he took the sight of Dover, wallowing under the bedclothes like a stranded whale, in his stride. Even the grubby, much-darned, blue and white army surplus pyjamas didn't distress him overmuch. Any man who has had the experience of finding a judge of the High Court dead on the floor of his rooms and clad only in a flowered bikini and a lady's rubber bathing cap is, sartorially speaking, pretty well immune to shock.

Mr Lickes's sensibilities were offended, however, by the frowzy atmosphere which Dover's lengthy occupation had engendered. He bounced over to the window and, without so much as a by-your-leave, succeeded in opening it at least half an inch.

Dover scowled fearfully and sank even farther beneath the sheets.

'That's better!' announced Mr Lickes and took up a position of rigid attention at the foot of the bed. Slowly he placed his hands on his hips and rose to the tips of his toes. 'You wanted to see me about the murder of Mr Chantry, I believe?'

'I suppose so,' came a glum and muffled voice from the bed.

The remark was followed by a deep sigh as Dover wondered where the hell to begin. 'Knew Chantry, did you?'

'Oh yes, of course. Everybody in Sully Martin knew Walter Chantry. He was one of the leading personalities in the village – the leading personality, I suppose.'

'Popular chap, was he?'

Mr Lickes considered this whilst inclining his trunk in a series of sharp jerks to the left. 'Yes, I think so. On the whole. Some people might have found him a bit overbearing but, on the other hand, he was a great one for getting things done.'

'What sort of things?'

'Oh, all sorts of things.'

Dover poked his head crossly out of the blankets. 'Don't give me any of that, laddie! If you want me to come over there and drag it out of you word by bloody word, I will – don't you fret!'

'I'm sorry,' apologized Mr Lickes who could have made mincemeat out of an unhealthy lump like Dover with both hands tied behind him. 'It's just that it's difficult to think of anything he wasn't involved in. He was president of this and chairman of that and patron of the other. You name it. Boy Scouts, the Old People's Welfare Committee, National Savings, Vicar's Warden at the church, the Library Committee . . . Mr Sully Martin, I suppose you could call him. My wife always used to say that he was after an MBE or something in the Honours List but, personally, I don't think it was just that. He was a very energetic man, you know, and he thoroughly enjoyed having a finger in every pie. He'd got some pretty big ideas for Sully Martin. If he'd had his way, he'd have put us on the map all right.'

'As what, for God's sake?' asked Dover, who had not been impressed by what he'd seen so far.

'Oh, a tourist centre.'

'A tourist centre?' Dover let fly with a nasty sort of laugh and pulled the sheets up even farther round his fat, police-man's neck. 'He must have been a bloody optimist!'

'Well, it was only going to be on quite a small scale. He wasn't planning to turn us into another Brighton or Stratford-on-Avon or anything. In fact, the tourists were going to be a sort of by-product, really. What he was actually after was to make Sully Martin a beautiful place to live in. You see, we've got the church, which is supposed to be a very fine one, and most of the houses are pretty old and basically rather charming. They just need doing up, that's all. And that's where poor old Chantry did run into a bit of opposition.'

Dover grunted a query.

'Money,' sighed Mr Lickes. 'The local people haven't got it and, even if they have, they're not going to spend it stripping their Tudor oak beams or painting their front doors yellow. And the gardens, too. They were a great source of contention. Mr Chantry wanted flowers and the cottagers wanted rows of beans with untidy bits of coloured paper to keep the birds off. From Chantry's point of view there was only one solution.' Mr Lickes paused for another grunt of interrogation but Dover was feeling mean and refused to oblige. Mr Lickes had no choice but to carry on. 'Get rid of the villagers,' he explained.

Dover yawned. 'How?'

'Buy them out and replace them with people who were ready and willing to spend a small fortune on conversions. Retired people, artists, writers, film stars – you know the sort of thing. It's been done in other places.'

'And Chantry would have made a packet out of it?'

'Well, one imagines that he didn't intend to lose on the transaction but things weren't quite as simple as that. You'd need a terrific amount of capital to do the whole thing properly and Chantry just didn't have it. He didn't want to let anybody else in on the scheme so he had to be content with making a modest start here and there. Wing Commander Pile's place, for example. Mr Chantry bought that up for about four hundred pounds, got the sitting tenant out, did it over and sold it to Pile for a cool four thousand.'

'That must have made him a few enemies.'

'Not murderous ones. Oh, some people had started mutter-ing about Rachmanism but that was a gross exaggeration. His ideas were always a jolly sight bigger than his means.'

With a considerable amount of puffing and blowing Dover hoisted himself into a sitting position and began wondering morosely if he was getting bed sores. 'Was he after this dump?' he asked.

'The Blenheim Towers?' Mr Lickes shot a wary glance at the unkempt figure in the bed who was now scratching himself luxuriously under the armpits. It didn't do, Mr Lickes re-minded himself, to underestimate people. This chap was a high-ranking detective from Scotland Yard and he couldn't possibly be as big a fool as he looked. On the contrary, to get away with this sort of behaviour, he must be a positive genius. Mr Lickes congratulated himself on having penetrated beneath the boorish exterior to the Great Detective lurking underneath. He was not, poor man, the first, nor would he be the last, to make this mistake.

'Yes,' said Dover, judging from Mr Lickes's hesitation that he had accidentally scored a bull's eye, 'the Blenheim Towers.' He leered invitingly. 'Why don't you sit down, laddie, and tell me all about it?'

Four

Mr Lickes, for reasons best known to himself, preferred to stand and twitch alternate calf muscles.

'Chantry, you and the Blenheim Towers,' prompted Dover, pressing home his advantage with all the vigour of a damp sponge.

Mr Lickes was becoming more and more impressed with the sheer devilish cunning of Dover's technique. 'Motels,' he said.

'Motels?'

'Mr Chantry was a great believer in motels. He thought they were the coming thing in the tourist industry. He was all for me turning the Blenheim Towers into one.'

'And?'

'Where would I find twenty-five thousand pounds? Don't get me wrong. I'm as eager as the next man to make a million but I'm not the tycoon type and I never shall be. Even if the scheme had been a roaring success, I should have been in hock to my bank manager or whoever it was advanced the money for the rest of my life. And if it wasn't a success – well,' – he shuddered as he thought about it – 'Mrs Lickes and I would have been out on the street, wouldn't we? The Blenheim Towers may not exactly be the Ritz but it is mine and I can cope with it. I kept telling Mr Chantry that.'

'But he wouldn't listen?'

'Too busy expounding his next bright idea,' said Mr Lickes, pulling a rather rueful face. 'That involved me selling out to one of the big hotel chains, getting them to convert us into a motel and putting me in charge of it as manager.'

'Sounds all right,' said Dover.

'All Mr Chantry's ideas sounded all right. It was only when you started looking into them that you saw the snags. Take this one, for example. No big hotel chain has ever shown the slightest interest in buying me out and they wouldn't make me manager if they did. I know how these things work. The best I could hope for was enough capital to go and buy myself another hotel somewhere. Well, as I said to Mr Chantry, why bother? I'm perfectly happy and contented here.'

'So he dropped the idea?'

'Not really. That's as far as we'd got before he was killed.'

Dover let his gaze wander wearily out of the window and tried to twist all this into a motive for murder. Was Mr Lickes the sort of man who would kill for the sake of a quiet life?

'It was upsetting my regulars, too,' said Mr Lickes, forcing his chin into his neck and squaring his shoulders.

'What was?'

'All this talk about converting the Blenheim Towers into a four-star motel. They could see themselves being turned out into the snow at a moment's notice. You'd never seen such a panic. I even had Mrs Boyle weeping on my shoulder so you can imagine what a state the others were in. And of course the more I told them I wasn't going to change anything, the less they believed me.'

Dover nodded, almost as though he was actually listening, and stared out of the window again. It was still raining.

Mr Lickes risked a surreptitious glance at his watch. He really was frightfully busy and, while it was one's undoubted business to assist the police in every way one could, one would prefer not to spend the whole day doing it. He waited a moment or two and then cleared his throat as loudly as he dared.

Dover dragged his eyes away from the window and looked blankly at Mr Lickes.

'Would you like me to tell you what I did on the night of the earthquake?' asked Mr Lickes hopefully.

Dover's bottom lip pouted out. It was all go. 'You might as well, I suppose.'

The permission was grudging but Mr Lickes seized it eagerly and began to rattle at great speed through his story. The first part was pretty much what Dover had been led to expect from Miss Kettering's evidence.

There had been the sudden, terrified awakening in the small hours as the earthquake shook the Blenheim Towers from attic to cellar. Then a few moments of bewilderment and near panic followed, in the case of Mr and Mrs Lickes, with a commendable concern for the safety of others. As soon as they gathered their wits, the pair of them rushed off to see that their guests were all right. Luckily they were, and Mr Lickes's anxiety spread to wider fields.

'I just had a sort of feeling,' he explained to Dover, 'that something terrible must have happened somewhere and, since we were comparatively unscathed, I felt free to go out and see if there was anything I could do. My wife decided to come with me.'

'How long after the earthquake?'

Mr Lickes hunched his shoulders. 'I'd have to guess – ten minutes, fifteen. Not much more, I don't think.'

'Go on.'

'Well, when we got out on to the drive, we could hear people shouting and screaming. It was coming from the direction of North Street and so we hurried off that way as quickly as we could. We'd had the foresight to bring a couple of torches with us and that proved a great help because, really, you could hardly see anything. I don't remember noticing anybody in our lane but when we turned into East Street there seemed to be a bit more activity. We could see people in the distance, up towards North Street, moving about with torches and there was a lot of shouting going on. No,' said Mr Lickes, cleverly anticipating the question that Dover should have asked, 'I didn't recognize anybody, not at that stage. Well, we'd got nearly to the top of East Street when we practically bumped into Wing Commander Pile and his daughter. They were in a terrible state. The girl was crying and as near hysterical as makes no difference and the wing commander's face was covered in blood. They were only wearing pyjamas, too, and it was pouring with rain and very cold. The wing commander told us that the roof of their house had come down on top of them and then we decided that the best thing would be for my wife to bring the girl back to the Blenheim Towers and put her to bed. I thought the wing commander should have gone with them but he refused. He said he wanted to go back to his house and try and salvage some of his belongings and get some clothes and things. After that, he was determined to help with the rescue work. I must confess I thought that was a quite unnecessary gesture, considering the state the chap was in, but he insisted. I suppose,' added Mr Lickes with a slightly disparaging sniff, 'it's the service training. Gives them a sense of duty.'

Dover gazed dully at Mr Lickes and offered no comment.

'Well,' continued Mr Lickes, giving the toes of his right foot a vigorous work-out, 'Wing Commander Pile and I got to where North Street crosses East Street and it was utter chaos. People were rushing about and shouting and screaming and there was this sort of awful gap where the top side of North Street had been. I can't tell you how dreadful it was.'

'Good,' said Dover briskly. 'Don't!'

Mr Lickes blinked. He was all for cutting things short but one does like one's efforts to be appreciated. He thought that detectives were supposed to bombard you with questions and demand the most detailed accounts. This specimen didn't even seem mildly interested in anything. 'Well,' he asked uncertainly, 'what is it you want to know?'

Dover blew his cheeks out with an air of hopelessness. 'Oh, who you saw and what you did,' he advised. 'Just cut out the hearts-and-flowers stuff.'

Hearts-and-flowers stuff? Mr Lickes supposed that included any description of the horrors and the suffering he had witnessed that terrible night. Oh well, if that's what Chief Inspector Dover wanted, he could have it. 'As far as I can remember, the first person I saw after I'd met up with Wing Commander Pile was one of those artist types from the place they call the Studio. That's the house in East Street opposite Mr Chantry's place.'

'Name?' said Dover.

'Oliver, Jim Oliver. He's the painter. The other man's a sculptor and the woman does pottery. Well, Jim Oliver was just coming out of their house. He'd got a spade he'd come back for. We were just asking him what was happening when young Hooper loomed up out of the darkness.' Mr Lickes glanced at Dover doubtfully. 'Colin Hooper is Mr Chantry's son-in-law,' he said.

'I know that!' snarled Dover. 'Get on with it!'

'Well, he told us that the worst part seemed to be over by the pub. He and Mr Chantry had been doing what they could in that area but they needed help. I volunteered to go back with him, and Wing Commander Pile said he'd join us as soon as he'd collected some clothes. Jim Oliver, though, said he and Lloyd Thomas had been trying to rescue a woman at the other end of North Street – that's why he'd come back for the spade – and so he'd have to get back there. Well, we split up then. Colin Hooper and I went off in the direction of the pub but, when we got as far as the cottages, I found young Mrs Jenkins trying to free her husband from a pile of bricks and things that had fallen across his legs. I stopped off to help her and Colin Hooper went on. I think he said something about joining his father-in-law. After that, I honestly don't remember noticing anybody much. We got Mr Jenkins free and his wife and I dragged him clear and then carried him off to the Studio. They've got a big sort of kitchen there and it sort of developed into a casualty clearing station. When I'd got Jenkins settled I went back to the cottages. I knew the people who lived in the middle one – the girl helps out in the kitchen for us when we're busy – and . . .'

'All right, you're a hero,' said Dover sourly. 'Me, I'm interested in Chantry.'

'I didn't see Mr Chantry.'

'Not at all?'

'Not at all.'

'But you were working in the same area.'

'Yes, but you've no idea what it was like. Everything had just slipped down the side of the hill. All you could do was scramble down in the dark and start pulling the debris away and shouting to see if there was anybody trapped underneath. It was heavy work and it took simply hours. You'd no time to bother about what anybody else was doing. I just got on with my bit and I suppose everybody else was the same.'

'Didn't you notice anybody?'

'Only the poor devils I was trying to pull out – and none of them was in any state to go around committing murder, I can tell you.'

Dover scowled. It was going to be one of those cases, all right. It'd take a miracle to sort this lot out and Dover knew, none better, how very few miracles had ever smiled on him. 'Did you see Chantry's son-in-law?' he asked, since Mr Lickes appeared to be waiting for him to say something.

Mr Lickes shook his head. 'Not until it was light and the police and everybody'd got up here. When they arrived and took over, most of the rest of us packed it in. We'd just about had it, you understand. My wife had set up a sort of canteen in Chantry's front garden and she and some of the other ladies were serving tea and sandwiches. I stopped off for a cup and I seem to remember that Colin Hooper was there, too. After that I came back to the hotel and had a quick bath and changed and then it was time to start dealing with the breakfasts. Life must go on, mustn't it?' Mr Lickes raised his arms above his head and drew in a deep breath.

Dover had a mind like a jumping bean and Mr Lickes's peculiar antics had been irritating him for some time. ' What do you keep wriggling about for?' he demanded.

' Isometrics,' replied Mr Lickes, delighted that they'd now moved on to a mutually interesting topic of conversation.

' You should see a doctor, laddie.'

Mr Lickes giggled. Fancy this surly-looking policeman having an impish sense of humour! ' A fellow likes to keep fit,' he explained, ' and this isometric system, suitably modified to meet my own personal requirements, does pretty well.'

' I should have thought you got enough blooming exercise just doing your own job,' observed Dover. ' I know I do.'

' Ah, I'm afraid a lot of people delude themselves into thinking that. It's a great mistake.' Mr Lickes ran a discerning eye over Dover's bulging form. ' I've got a few books I could lend you, if you like.'

' Don't bother,' growled Dover.

Mr Lickes understood his attitude perfectly. ' No, well it's not everybody's idea of the perfect system,' he agreed. ' It's not even mine, come to that. I'm really a great believer in jogging. You know, out in the fresh air in all weathers with the wind and the rain in your face, just jogging happily along. I used to find that a steady five or six miles a day kept me in perfect condition. However, in the circumstances, I thought it better to give it up for a while.'

' In what circumstances?' asked Dover who'd already classified Mr Lickes as a chronic nut-case some time ago.

Mr Lickes's mouth twisted bitterly. ' There were complaints,' he said. ' Well, only one really. You wouldn't think people would be so narrow-minded in this day and age, would you? My apparel may have been scanty but it was not indecent. And to be accused of being a Peeping Tom into the bargain!' Mr Lickes drew himself up with a fastidious shudder. 'A man in my position has no defence against that kind of slander.'

'A Peeping Tom?' Dover found this sort of thing much more diverting than any lousy old murder investigation. 'Who called you that, eh?'

'You may well ask! As a matter of fact, it was Wing Commander Pile. As I explained to him, I'd been jogging around this village after supper for more years than I can remember without a single complaint from anybody. Then he moves down here and I'm accused of being an exhibitionist and a *voyeur* of a particularly nasty kind.'

'No!' said Dover encouragingly.

'I thought you'd find it hard to credit,' agreed Mr Lickes. 'It was his daughter, you see. I used to go via Cherry Lane and West Street and out through the old Sally Gate, down the main road and back round through Sidle Alley. Well, by that time I was usually feeling a bit puffed and I used to stop for a few moments to get my second wind. Miss Pile's bedroom was at the back of the house, overlooking Sidle Alley, and Wing Commander Pile had the infernal cheek to accuse me of pausing there to watch her undress. I ask you! Of course, one understands his concern for the poor girl but, even so . . .' Mr Lickes shuddered again and looked at his watch. 'Good heavens, is that the time? Well, if you have no further questions, Mr Dover, I really have rather a lot to do downstairs so . . .'

Unlike her husband, Mrs Lickes was only too glad to sit down and have a bit of a rest. She was a frail, tired looking woman who accepted, perhaps a little too readily, the dictum that the customer is always right.

'I put her in one of the spare bedrooms,' she told Dover, referring to Wing Commander Pile's daughter. 'She'd a few bruises and cuts but I thought the best thing I could do was to get her settled and off to sleep as soon as possible. Of course, if she'd been a normal sort of girl, you could have perhaps found something for her to do to take her mind off things – I've always found there's nothing like hard work to stop you worrying – but with her being like she is – well, I didn't quite know what to do. I mean, I've never had any experience of people like that before. I wasn't too happy about just leaving her all on her own in a strange bed but things looked such a mess round North Street that I really felt I ought to go back there and help out. I did wonder about asking one of our ladies to look after her but, well, you don't like to trouble your guests, not with a thing like that, do you? In the end I gave her a couple of my sleeping tablets. That put her out like a light and she slept right through until gone lunch time. By the way, before I forget, what time would you like your afternoon tea?'

'Four o'clock,' said Dover promptly, grateful to find somebody at last who'd got their priorities right.

Mrs Lickes nodded and went on with her story. How she'd made a gallon or so of sweet tea and put it in an old milk churn they happened to have, and how she'd lugged that plus an enormous pile of sandwiches, another torch and a couple of old sheets for bandages all the way back to North Street. She reckoned that, what with one thing and another, she must have been away for about an hour.

'I saw them taking some of the wounded into the Studio so that's where I went first of all. It was terrible in there. All these poor people lying about on the floor, bleeding and moaning. This Wittgenstein woman – she makes vases and things – she was doing the best she could but there is a limit, isn't there? I mean with first aid. I'm always afraid you might be doing more harm than good, fiddling around.

'Well, I suppose it must have been about half past four when some proper medical people turned up and I thought they could manage without me for a bit and so I went back outside again. To tell you the truth, I was worried about Mr Lickes. He's got to be awfully careful, you know. Any heavy work and he ricks that back of his before you can say knife. I know people think he's awfully strong with his physical fitness and all those muscles and everything, but I've learned better than to take any chances with him. Oh – that reminds me – I haven't got the coal in for the lounge fire yet. Coal fires look ever so nice but they do make a of work, don't they?'

There was a pause and Dover opened his eyes to find Mrs Lickes gazing expectantly at him. He made a valiant attempt at bridging the hiatus. 'Oh, quite,' he said.

Mrs Lickes appeared to be awaiting more.

Dover silently damned the stupid cow to all eternity and tried again. 'Now then – er – when you were doing this Florence Nightingale stuff . . .'

'In the Studio? Yes?'

'Er – did you see What's-his-name?'

'Mr Chantry? No, I don't think so.'

'Oh, 'strewth!' snapped Dover crossly, 'You're worse than your blooming husband! Can't you remember, for God's sake?'

Mrs Lickes, more than a little taken aback by this onslaught, couldn't. She began making excuses. It had been dark in the Studio – did Mr Dover realize that the electricity had all gone off and they had to manage with a couple of old oil lamps? – and then, of course, people had looked such a mess that it was almost impossible to recognize anybody. The men in particular had their faces and clothes absolutely caked in mud.

A sideways peep at Dover's implacable visage warned Mrs Lickes that she would have to do better than this. She managed a few more feeble remarks about being fully occupied with the frightened and injured victims of the earthquake and then let her voice trail guiltily away.

Dover emitted an elaborate sigh of exasperation. 'Oh, all right,' he snarled, ' though, if you ask me, there's none so blind as those trying to conceal evidence from the police. Now, get on with it! I've got something better to do with my time than listen to you imitating a babbling brook. You left this Studio place. Then what?'

Mrs Lickes gulped back her tears and told herself it was probably just his way of putting things. 'Well,' she resumed, 'I thought I'd better go into what was left of North Street. Everybody had been saying that's where the worst damage was and I knew I'd find Mr Lickes right in the thick of things. Well, when I got round the corner, I saw that there were a lot of people gathered in Mr Chantry's front garden. I went in to ask if any of them had seen Mr Lickes and then I found that Millie Hooper was there, making cups of tea and things. They have Calor gas, you see, so they were all right. Well, somebody said they'd seen Mr Lickes only half an hour or so earlier so I thought he was all right and I decided to stay and give Millie Hooper a hand. Poor girl, she was looking so peaked. She's expecting, you know, and with all that standing around . . . Well, it started getting light and more and more police and demolition men and first-aid people kept arriving, so our local people began knocking off. I caught sight of Mr Lickes and I insisted that he came straight back here to the hotel. He catches cold so easily and he was absolutely soaked to the skin, poor thing. I meant to follow him in a few minutes, of course, because the WVS had got a proper canteen going in the Church Hall and we were running out of food and things anyhow. But, it was Millie Hooper, you see. She'd only just begun to think about what her father was going to say when he got back and found she'd given away every scrap of food and drink they had in the house. Mr Chantry wasn't a mean man, not really, but he was what you might call careful. I know Millie Hooper had to account to him for every last penny of her housekeeping allowance. Well, the more she thought about it, the more upset she got. In the end I decided to hang on for a bit so I could put a good word in for her when he finally turned up.'

A violent creaking of the bed springs warned Mrs Lickes that Detective Chief Inspector Dover was rousing himself to put a question.

' Frightened of her father, was she?'

' Frightened?' Mrs Lickes gave a rather uncharitable laugh. ' She was terrified of him! Just like her poor dead mother, if you really want to know.'

' Why?'

'He was a hard man. Hard in business and hard in his private life. He never accepted excuses. He'd got very high standards and he expected other people, especially his family, to live up to them. Millie Hooper's twenty-one, you know, and right up to the time she got married she had to be home every night by ten o'clock. The poor girl was the laughing stock of the village. There isn't another teenager in the place who was treated like that. It meant she couldn't go to the pictures in Beccles or dances or anything. She'd no life at all, poor kid. We all thought she'd finish up an old maid, waiting on her father hand and foot until he passed on but then, all of a sudden, Colin Hooper appeared on the scene. I wouldn't exactly call him a knight in shining armour but at least he was a bit of support for Millie's side.' Mrs Lickes glanced at Dover slyly. ' Well, that's what we thought he was going to be. They've been married nearly six months now and, I must say, he's not put up all that much of a show so far. Mind you, he's in a very difficult position. He was working for Mr Chantry when he met Millie and now he's a junior partner in the business. That was Mr Chantry's wedding present to them. Naturally, they had to pay for it. No question of a house of their own, you see. Mr Chantry insisted on them living with him. Well, it's a big house, isn't it? Plenty of room for everybody.'

Dover was now beginning to sit up and take notice. His fat, pasty face assumed an almost happy expression as, for the first time on this lousy case, he felt solid ground beneath his feet. A disgruntled, down-trodden daughter! Now, that was something a chap could get his teeth into!

Dover's approach to murder cases was crudely simple. Husbands were murdered by their wives and wives by their husbands. If they weren't, he rapidly lost interest in the face of the additional work likely to be involved in pinning the crime on somebody else. Occasionally, of course, even Dover was forced to adjust his ideas. Some murder victims hadn't got a spouse to cop it for them and the chief inspector was obliged to look elsewhere. That's when children proved such a blessing.

He addressed Mrs Lickes with unaccustomed delicacy. 'This fellow Chantry was rolling in it, was he?'

'I believe he was quite nicely off,' admitted Mrs Lickes, who had more than an inkling of where Dover's thoughts were wending. 'He wasn't short of the odd shilling, that's for sure. He was the biggest builder round these parts and those property deals of his in the village must have brought in quite a pretty penny.'

'And his daughter's the sole heir, eh?'

'I should imagine so. She was his only child and his wife's been dead for a long time now. Millie Hooper will come in for the lot, if you ask me – the business and everything.'

'Who'll run the business now?'

Mrs Lickes avoided Dover's eye as she put the boot in. 'Well, Colin Hooper will, won't he? That's what everybody in the village is assuming. There were only two partners, you see. Him and poor Mr Chantry.'

'It's an ill wind,' said Dover with patent cunning.

Mrs Lickes was forced to agree. 'Young people are so impatient these days,' she sighed. 'They don't want to wait for anything. Of course,' she added hurriedly, 'I don't for one moment believe that Millie Hooper would have harmed a hair of her father's head. She was quite fond of him, really. Besides, she wouldn't have been up to it physically, would she?'

'You're putting your money on the husband, are you?'

'Certainly not!' Mrs Lickes endeavoured to look as though butter wouldn't melt in her mouth. 'They're a very nice young couple, both of them, and I'm sure they'd never dream of hurting a fly. All I'm saying is that I just don't see Millie Hooper having the strength to murder a grown man in the middle of an earthquake. She's six months pregnant, you know, and by all accounts she's not having an easy time of it. Of course, she's always been a rather sickly-looking little thing.'

For once in his life Dover put two and two together and got the right answer. 'Six months?' he repeated. 'I thought you just said she hadn't been married as long as six months?'

Mrs Lickes lowered her eyes. 'I was only speaking in round numbers,' she said. 'Of course, with Millie Hooper being so enormous, you do tend to think she's further gone than she actually is.'

''Strewth,' guffawed Dover, 'they must have hit the blooming jackpot pretty quick!'

'I suppose in their case there was nothing much to wait for,' murmured Mrs Lickes. 'Most young couples have got all kinds of financial problems and nowhere proper to live. The Hoopers hadn't any problems on that score.'

Dover sniggered. 'Maybe they jumped the gun a bit, eh?'

Having, at last, got Dover under starter's orders, Mrs Lickes could afford to wax indignant. 'I don't know what you mean!' she protested. 'Millie Hooper isn't that kind of girl at all.'

'It's these innocent ones that usually get caught.'

'They don't get caught if they don't do something wrong in the first place,' retorted Mrs Lickes hotly. 'And Millie Hooper just wouldn't have dared. Her father would have killed her. Why, if he'd suspected for one second that that baby had been conceived out of wedlock, he'd have thrown Millie and her husband out of that house so quick their feet wouldn't have touched the ground!'

Five

Dover had hoped to make it downstairs to the bathroom and back before the next witness arrived but things took a little longer than he had anticipated. He laboured, panting and blaspheming, up the precipitous stairs to find a grim-faced Wing Commander Pile already standing bolt upright in the middle of the bedroom.

'I believe,' said Wing Commander Pile, squinting disdainfully down his nose, 'that you wished to see me.'

Dover removed his overcoat and dropped it by the side of his bed. 'Got to see all the murder suspects,' he explained as he bent down to kick off his unlaced boots. 'Where's the girl?'

Wing Commander Pile's closely shaven jaw tightened as he watched Dover clamber back into bed and tug the sheets up. 'You are not proposing to conduct this interview on your back, I trust?' he asked icily.

'I can understand you being surprised,' grunted Dover, digging about under the bedclothes for something that was sticking into him. 'Most men in my state of health'd be in hospital, not flogging themselves to a shadow doing their duty. Of course,' – he brought out a piece of toast and examined it

morosely – 'that's always been my trouble – too bloody conscientious.' He sighed and shoved the piece of toast in his
mouth. 'Where did you say the girl was?'

'Linda is downstairs in her room and that is where she is
going to stay.'

'But I want to see her.'

'So I have gathered. Unfortunately, I cannot permit it.'

Dover goggled and gulped down the last of the toast. 'Why
the hell not?'

'My daughter may have the appearance of a mature woman
but she has the mind of a child. You would not, I imagine,
cross-examine a five-year-old girl about a murder.'

'Kids have been questioned before,' objected Dover. 'Of
course, it needs handling with tact and delicacy by an expert
but . . .'

'What has happened in other cases is of no concern to me.
I have my daughter's interests to consider and I have no intention of standing idly by while you revive memories whose
horrors are now mercifully beginning to fade into the back-
ground.'

''Strewth,' Dover grumbled, 'I'm not going to eat the girl!'

Wing Commander Pile remained perfectly calm. 'You are
not going to interview her, either. I don't know how far your
powers extend, chief inspector, but I am fully prepared to
make an issue of this. I have already been in touch with
Linda's medical advisers and they all, without exception, agree
that she should not be subjected to any form of police interrogation.'

Dover sighed. This joker spelt trouble. He looked the sort
of bastard who not only knew all his own rights but everybody
else's as well. Of course, in normal circumstances, Dover would
have flattened him quicker than that but, what with his stomach
and this cold . . . A somewhat tatty olive branch was offered.
'I'd have no objection to you being present.'

Wing Commander Pile contented himself with a curt shake
of his head.

'It is a murder case,' Dover pointed out dejectedly.

'My daughter could tell you nothing which would help you in your enquiries. She was well away from the scene when Mr Chantry was killed.'

'Oh?' said Dover, rallying a bit. 'And how do you know when Chantry was killed?'

'I don't – but it was certainly after Mrs Lickes had escorted Linda back to this hotel.' Wing Commander Pile expertly and effortlessly swung a chair into precisely the right position and seated himself upon it with a crisp economy of movement. 'When you are ready, I will make my statement.'

'I'm ready now,' said Dover.

Wing Commander Pile's eyebrows rose. 'Aren't you going to take notes?'

'Notes?' Dover sank back with a suppressed groan of fury. What did this snooty beggar think he was – a bloody short-hand-typist? 'I have a sergeant to take notes!' he growled.

'But your sergeant isn't here.'

'He never bloody well is when he's wanted,' snarled Dover. 'Still, it makes no odds. I've got a photographic memory.'

Wing Commander Pile's eyebrows went higher.

'It's true!' insisted Dover, over-elaborating his lies as usual. 'You ask anybody up at the Yard. I'm famous for it. They call me What's-his-name of the Metropolitan Police.'

'I can well believe it.'

'So you don't have to worry.' Dover laughed with touching modesty and tapped himself on the forehead. 'Anything you say'll be stored up here. Word for word. Like one of those computer things. Now, you just go right ahead and tell me what happened. Start from the earthquake.'

'Well,' – Wing Commander Pile frowned as he marshalled his thoughts before recording them for ever in the self-proclaimed human memory bank – 'we were in bed, of course. Asleep. I suppose the first tremors partially woke me up but, before I could realize what was happening, my bed, the bedroom, the whole house appeared to slide and then tip over

69

towards the rear. Then I heard this ominous cracking sound over my head and somehow I knew that the roof was collapsing. One does have these peculiar flashes of comprehension in moments of crisis – I've noticed it before. Well, I remember calling out – a warning to Linda, I suppose – and the next minute the entire ceiling just fell down on top of me. I lost consciousness. Something hit me on the head, I think. A tile? A beam? I don't know. I don't think I was knocked out for more than a minute or two. When I came back to my senses I found myself buried under all this debris and rubbish. I was just beginning to try and free myself when I heard somebody shouting my name.' The wing commander paused to let the suspense build up. ' It was Walter Chantry.'

Dover, who was desperate to get his own back, didn't even open his eyes.

'Walter Chantry!' repeated Wing Commander Pile. ' He saved my life. It is thanks to him, and to him alone, that I am sitting here today.'

Dover refrained from comment.

' I am making it my business,' Wing Commander Pile went on grandly, ' to get a posthumous George Medal for him. I feel it's the least I can do.'

' He ought to get something,' agreed Dover. ' Well, what happened next?'

' I called out to Chantry not to bother about me but to help Linda. He shouted back that he had already got her out and that she was all right.' Wing Commander Pile broke off his narrative to stare suspiciously at Dover. ' You are taking all this in, I hope?'

The chief inspector, suddenly envisaging letters of complaint winging their way straight to the Assistant Commissioner (Crime), opened his eyes and assumed an expression of alert intelligence. ' Every word,' he assured Wing Commander Pile earnestly.

' Good,' came the stern reply, ' because I can promise you I have no intention of repeating it. Well, I then heard Mr

Chantry scrambling in through the window – most of the glass had already fallen out – and he started trying to extricate me. Eventually, he succeeded. I cannot emphasize Mr Chantry's bravery too much. The back part of the house had already gone and the part I was trapped in could have collapsed at any moment. It is not every man who, in that terrifying darkness, would have risked his own life to save that of a friend.'

Dover's facial muscles were already beginning to ache with the unaccustomed exercise but he nodded his head unflinchingly and urged the wing commander to continue.

'There's little more to say. Mr Chantry assisted me outside and I joined Linda who, very distressed and bewildered, was waiting for me on the pavement. Naturally I was chiefly concerned with her welfare but I did, thank God, thank Walter Chantry most sincerely. Just as I was expressing my gratitude, rather incoherently I fear, we heard cries coming from the direction of the public house by the old Sally Gate. All the buildings in that direction seemed to have disappeared, as far as one could tell through the rain and the darkness, but there were these cries. Immediately Walter Chantry, with a resolution typical of the man, broke into my speech of thanks and said that he must go and do what he could to help the other victims of this terrible disaster. I attempted to dissuade him – the hazardous nature of the operation was self-evident – but to no avail. He hurried off into the night.'

'Did you see him again?' asked Dover.

'I did not. At that time Linda was my first concern. She was only wearing a nightdress and, as we could hear more buildings collapsing around us, I began to lead her away from the danger area. We had barely gone more than a few yards when we encountered Mr and Mrs Lickes.'

'Yes, I know all about that.' Dover had met some pompous bores in his time but he reckoned Wing Commander Pile took the biscuit. 'Mrs Lickes brought your daughter back here and you returned to your house to get some clothes or something. And Chantry's son-in-law turned up, didn't he?'

'That is correct. Mr Chantry had sent him back to get some assistance. Lickes went off with him and I returned to my house to salvage what I could in the way of clothes for myself and Linda. I had intended then to join Mr Chantry but there seemed to be a lot of noise and confusion coming from the opposite direction. I went over there to see what was happening and the chaos I found was quite unbelievable. It was only to be expected, of course. Civilians have very little idea of proper organization. What was lacking was firm overall control and direction. That sort of thing is somewhat less glamorous than digging through piles of stones and bricks with your bare hands but it was absolutely essential in the kind of emergency we were faced with.' Wing Commander Pile's face took on a glow of noble self-sacrifice. 'Since I had the experience, I felt I had no choice but to take control until the proper authorities arrived.'

'Bully for you,' said Dover.

'I am glad you think so. Others, unfortunately, were not so appreciative.'

Dover was sympathetic. He'd been accused of shirking too often himself not to understand what it felt like. 'There's always some unco-operative bastard standing around and criticizing,' he observed.

Wing Commander Pile agreed. 'There were several that night,' he said grimly. 'However, it is not my habit to be deflected from doing my duty by petty jealousy. I made a quick appreciation and came to the conclusion that the area on the far side of East Street was the one on which we should concentrate. The damage was nothing like so severe there, but that merely meant that the prospects of finding survivors were enhanced. I set about organizing my working parties and continued directing the operations in that area for the rest of the night.'

'So you didn't see Chantry again?'

'No. I assumed he was still working over Sally Gate area. When I was relieved of my command responsibilities by the arrival of the professional squads, I naturally made my way directly back here to the Blenheim Towers. I still had Linda to consider.'

'Hm.' Dover heaved himself up in bed and tried to think of something keen and penetrating to say. 'Was Chantry a friend of yours?'

Wing Commander Pile considered the question with the solemnity of a High Court judge. 'Yes, I think you could say that he was. Not an intimate friend, perhaps, but a friend none the less. I have only been living in Sully Martin for a few months and Mr Chantry was one of the first people I met. I bought my house from him, as a matter of fact. Our business relations were extremely cordial and, as I got to know him better, my respect for him grew. He was a man of real integrity, moral stature and strength of character. I may tell you, chief inspector, that those are qualities for which I have the highest regard. It is the tragedy of modern society that it has lost all sense of decency and honour. You may have heard that Mr Chantry had great plans for Sully Martin? Ah – I imagined that Mr Lickes would have something to say on that subject. Well, you must understand that Mr Chantry was not only, or even primarily, concerned with bricks and mortar and landscape gardening. He wanted to create an environment of moral beauty as well. This, he knew, was not going to be easy to achieve. There are subversive elements in this village which must be torn out by the roots. Immoral elements! Don't let the smooth exterior of Sully Martin mislead you! Beneath the surface is filth! There are people in our midst who, in happier days, would have been burnt at the stake. Perverts, fornicators, adulterers!'

Dover wriggled uncomfortably. He was dying for a cup of tea and he resented being addressed as though he was a revivalist meeting. Blimey, fancy getting worked up into a muck sweat over a bit of bucolic slap and tickle! The pompous git ought to thank his lucky stars he'd nothing more serious to worry about.

Wing Commander Pile extracted a spotless white handkerchief from his sleeve and wiped the palms of his hands. 'I don't want you to think I am exaggerating,' he went on in a calmer voice, 'but I am quite convinced in my own mind that this is why Mr Chantry was killed. He had made enemies. Those who attack sin and the forces of darkness frequently do. They seized their opportunity and struck him down.'

'Who?' asked Dover shortly.

'I beg your pardon?'

'Let's have a few names, mate! Vague accusations don't amount to a row of tuppenny damns in my job.'

'I am not making any accusations,' countered Wing Commander Pile quickly. 'I was merely indicating an area which you might find fruitful to investigate further.'

'Who was Chantry sticking his knife into in particular?'

Wing Commander Pile ran his tongue over his lips. 'I don't know that I really care to mention any specific person.'

'You can stuff that!' roared Dover, highly delighted at being able to browbeat the wing commander in a good cause. 'I want facts!'

'One has no wish to be sued for defamation of character.'

'Defamation of character, my Aunt Fanny! Look, you want whoever snuffed Chantry out caught, don't you?'

'Of course.'

'Well, start singing then! There's nothing to worry about. Whatever you tell me'll stay within these four walls.'

'I have your word on that?'

'Cross my heart and hope to die!'

'Very well.' Wing Commander Pile capitulated with an air worthy of a defeated general surrendering his sword. 'I accept that I have a moral obligation. I owe it to poor Chantry's memory to . . .'

'Tell me!' screamed Dover.

'You've heard of the Studio?'

Dover frowned. 'Where this first-aid centre was?'

'That is the place. Ironically, it was poor Chantry himself who was responsible for importing those dreadful people into the village. He had some rather naïve ideas about artists, I'm afraid. He thought an artists' colony would give tone to the place and be an additional tourist attraction. He also had some vague notion that they would enrich the social life of our small community here. Well, to cut a long story short, he acquired the house which is now known as the Studio and did it up. There was no question of selling it, of course. Even poor Chantry realized that artists have no capital, so he decided to rent it. I believe it was the villain called Oliver who turned up in answer to the advertisement. He managed to convince Mr Chantry that he was a respectable citizen of good moral and financial standing and was granted a long and very advantageous lease on the property. This happened over a year ago, you understand, before I had moved into Sully Martin. Otherwise I might have been able to give Mr Chantry the benefit of my somewhat wider experience of this type of person. Well, no doubt you can guess for yourself what happened. Within a matter of weeks Oliver was not only behind with his rent but he had imported two more layabouts to join him. Permanently, that is. On high days and holidays, of course, threequarters of the scum of Chelsea move in.'

'Chelsea?' queried Dover.

'Or wherever these parasites hang out nowadays. However, we needn't bother about them at the moment. On the night of the earthquake only the three principal ruffians were in residence. Oliver himself, a woman called Wittgenstein and another man – Lloyd Thomas.'

'And you reckon this bunch had a grudge against Chantry?' asked Dover, trying to speed things up. According to his stomach it was getting time for his afternoon tea.

'They certainly had. It wasn't long, you realize, before poor Chantry knew he had made a terrible mistake. It wasn't only the fact that they weren't paying their rent. There was the public scandal of the way they were living.' Wing Commander

Pile looked cautiously round to make sure that his next remarks would not be overheard. 'The woman is cohabiting with *both* the men!'

'Go on!' said Dover.

'They make no secret of it. And sometimes' – the wing commander had another quick glance round – 'they all three sleep in the same bed!'

'Never!' said Dover, successfully repressing a chuckle.

'Then there's their nudity. Half the time they wander around without a stitch of clothing on.'

'That must liven village life up a bit!' snorted Dover.

Wing Commander Pile regarded him severely. 'Some of us do not find such licentious behaviour amusing, chief inspector. We have to think of its effect on the younger generation.'

'Oh, quite,' agreed Dover smarmily. 'Do they get up to any other high jinks?'

'They have orgies,' said Wing Commander Pile. 'Drunken orgies. Practically every night. Their record player is blaring until the small hours three or four times a week. I imagine they take drugs, too. They are typical degenerates in every conceivable way. Mr Chantry, with my full support, was determined to get rid of them. Just asking them to go had proved to be a complete waste of time.'

Dover had a one-track mind. 'Drunken orgies?' he murmured thoughtfully to himself.

'Just before he died, Mr Chantry had embarked upon more drastic action. He had consulted his solicitor. Decent, law-abiding, God-fearing people still have some rights, you know. Mr Chantry was determined to exercise them. You can take it from me, he would have left no stone unturned. Oliver and his crew realized this, of course, and they removed Chantry before he, poor fellow, had time to remove them.'

'*Drunken* orgies!' muttered Dover, hardly able to believe his good luck.

Wing Commander Pile misunderstood his interest. 'You may well be shocked, chief inspector. One doesn't associate

Sully Martin with hippies.' He pronounced the word with evident distaste.

'One certainly doesn't,' agreed Dover absently. 'Tell me, what do they drink? Beer or the hard stuff?'

'I'm afraid I have no idea. Does it matter?'

'No,' said Dover, 'I don't reckon it does, not really.'

The arrival of Miss Kettering with Dover's afternoon tea broke up the session and Wing Commander Pile, having unbeknowingly disgorged a vital piece of information, was allowed to take his leave.

'That's a rum kettle of fish,' said Dover, slobbering happily over the goodies on his tray.

Miss Kettering had sat down to recover her breath and was thrilled at being made the recipient of the Great Detective's confidences. 'Poor man, I feel so sorry for him,' she sighed, knowing how well the sympathetic little woman went down with most men. 'He's taken Mr Chantry's tragic death very much to heart.'

'Can't think why,' said Dover, licking the jam spoon nice and clean before replacing it in the pot.

'Oh well, they were birds of a feather, dear! They both thought the world was hurtling to eternal damnation and it was so nice for them to have somebody to talk to about it. Wing Commander Pile is going to be very lonely now, I'm afraid. He's not a very good mixer. Of course, he's got Linda but she can't really be much of a companion, can she?'

'Where's the wife?'

'She died when Linda was just a tiny baby, I believe, dear. He's had the whole burden to bear by himself. What that man has sacrificed just doesn't bear thinking about. We mustn't be surprised if he's a little difficult every now and again.'

'I've got past being surprised at anything,' said Dover as he wiped the crumbs off his chin with one corner of the sheet.

'Ah,' cooed Miss Kettering admiringly, 'that's because you've got such a well-balanced personality.'

Dover found himself warming to Miss Kettering. 'That's

77

very perceptive of you,' he rumbled. 'It's not everybody who notices.'

'I doubt if I would myself a year or so ago,' admitted Miss Kettering modestly. 'It's only since I took up the study of the occult that I've found true insight. Take the tarot cards, for instance. You've no idea how rewarding a session with those can be, and how comforting. Then there's numerology. Of course, I haven't actually got to that – it doesn't come till Lesson Fifteen – but I'm certain it's going to be a tremendous experience. I suppose,' – she looked at Dover rather wistfully – 'I suppose they don't encourage you to use divination in your work?'

Dover choked over his tea.

Miss Kettering nodded understandingly. 'There's a lot of blind antagonism about. I come across it myself, you know. You should hear Mrs Boyle on the subject. Talk about prejudice! Do you know, I once went to a great deal of trouble to concoct a really powerful charm against rheumatism for her and what did she do? She flung it back in my face! Nasty old cow! From the way she went on you'd have thought I was trying to put the evil eye on her.'

'You can take the tray,' said Dover. Miss Kettering might be a woman of rare understanding but he wasn't going to have her galloping her hobby-horses round his bedroom.

'Good heavens, have you finished already?' Miss Kettering jumped up and obediently accepted the tray. 'Well, that's a good sign. You must be feeling better if you can eat like that.'

Dover plumped up his pillows. 'I might get up a bit later on,' he said as he snuggled down.

Miss Kettering glanced at him anxiously. 'You don't want to overdo things,' she warned, 'not with your responsibilities.'

'I'll watch it,' promised Dover drowsily.

Sully Martin's church clock was striking a quarter past five when MacGregor came striding up the driveway back to the

Blenheim Towers. He found it most inconvenient, breaking off his investigations like this, but Dover tended to get very niggly if he was left alone for too long. For the umpteenth time Mac-Gregor pondered on the progress that could be achieved if only he hadn't got the dead weight of that lump of lard tied round his neck. Well – take this afternoon, for instance. All that careful questioning of people who had, quite understandably, been too bewildered and frightened almost to know what day of the week it was. The patience, the professional skill that had been needed to trace their movements and establish times. The endless checking and cross-checking. Could Dover have done it? Would Dover have done it? Like hell!

What would he have made of the Burkes, for example? Mr and Mrs Burke, having slaved away like demons, were sure that they had got Grandad outside by a quarter past two. Grandad, pinned down by the wardrobe across his bed, was vindictively certain that it was a good half hour later – and only then when they'd rescued the television set.

Or Jamie Pearson? He insisted that he'd been pulled clear by the Archangel Gabriel but his brother reckoned it was only their next-door neighbour armed with a tyre lever. What, Mac-Gregor couldn't forbear from asking himself, would Dover have made of Jamie Pearson? Or of any of them, come to that?

MacGregor couldn't forbear from providing the answer, either: sweet Fanny Adams, that's what Dover would have made of it. Dover liked a straight answer to a straight question and could turn very nasty if he didn't get it. Not for him the patient sifting through muddled statements and vague impressions. He preferred a more direct approach. Such as picking on somebody who wouldn't fight back and thumping a confession out of him.

Oh well, MacGregor comforted himself, on this occasion at least the old fool did seem to be confining himself to a comparatively passive role. Provided his imaginary cold didn't get better and the rain didn't stop, there was an outside chance that the murderer of Walter Chantry might actually be brought to book. For one of Chief Inspector Wilfred Dover's cases, it would make a welcome change.

Pausing only to find out from Mr Lickes what was on the menu for supper, MacGregor bounded up the stairs to Dover's room and knocked on the door. From inside came a sound akin to that of a blue-nosed whale clearing its blowhole and Mac-Gregor obediently entered.

Dover was putting his trousers on. It was not a very edifying sight and MacGregor, who was rather squeamish, averted his eyes.

'You're getting up, sir?' he asked with a foolishness that was meat and drink to Dover.

'No, you bloody fool,' came the sparkling reply, 'I'm stripping off to fight for the World Heavyweight Championship!'

MacGregor counted up to ten. 'I'm glad you're feeling better, sir.'

'I'll bet! Shove my shirt over!'

'This, sir?' MacGregor picked up a garment which seemed to have developed a bad case of fungi round the armpits.

'Those artists that live in the Studio,' said Dover, abandoning the unequal struggle with the top button of his trousers and grabbing his shirt from MacGregor's fastidious fingers.

'Oh, yes, sir. I interviewed them this afternoon.' Mac-Gregor pulled his notebook out and flipped over the pages. 'Two men and a woman, wasn't it? They turned their place into a first-aid shelter and . . .'

'I'm going to see 'em after I've had my dinner.'

'Tonight, sir?'

'No,' snarled Dover, the wit still scintillating, 'a week come Pancake Tuesday!'

'But I fixed up for the Hoopers to come in to see you this evening, sir.'

'Then you'll have to unfix it, won't you? I'll deal with them tomorrow, after lunch.'

'I'm not sure if that will be convenient, sir,' said MacGregor doubtfully.

Dover was busy scraping the varnish off a chair as he tied his bootlaces. 'It'll bloody well have to be!'

MacGregor frowned. What was the gibbering idiot up to now, for heaven's sake? The artists – Oliver, Lloyd Thomas and Wittgenstein – had seemed innocuous enough. Why was Dover suddenly taking an interest in them? If he had been dealing with anybody else, MacGregor would simply have asked but it was no good trying to do things the easy way with Dover. Extracting information from him required the subtlety of a Machiavelli. MacGregor got his cigarette case out and offered it as a preliminary sweetener.

Dover, who would have accepted a buckshee fag from a bloodstained multiple murderer (and on one occasion actually had), flopped back on the bed and puffed happily away while he waited for his soft nancy of a sergeant to make his next move.

'Perhaps,' began MacGregor, very nonchalantly, 'we ought just to bring each other up to date on the day's activities, sir? We've got half an hour or so before supper and then I can write the reports up later on tonight. Now' – he opened his notebook again – 'how many people did you see this afternoon, sir?'

'Three,' said Dover amiably. 'Lickes and his better half, and that chap, Pile. How many did you get through?'

'Er – twenty-four, sir, actually.'

Dover ground the odious comparison ruthlessly out of sight. 'You must have done a pretty skimpy job.'

'Not really, sir. I was able to eliminate most of them after a couple of minutes.'

'Didn't you turn up anything interesting?'

MacGregor reluctantly shook his head. 'I'm afraid not, sir. Of course I haven't had time to correlate my findings properly yet but it does look as though we can forget about ninety per cent of those I saw. Whole families can alibi each other, you see, and then some of the people were hurt in the earthquake and in no position to walk, never mind go around strangling Mr Chantry. And then, when you take into account all the children and the old people . . . Unless we're up against a conspiracy, sir, I'm sure most of them can be eliminated.'

'And those who can't?'

'Well, funnily enough, sir, those artists you want to see couldn't produce much in the way of alibis. Under the prevailing conditions there's nothing surprising about that, of course. They were wandering around, helping with the rescue work. Theoretically, one of them could have slipped off and killed Chantry. It needn't have taken more than a few minutes. Everybody's so vague about whom they saw and when they saw them, you see. I didn't come across much in the way of motive either.' MacGregor paused expectantly. 'Er – did you, sir?'

Dover was too leery a fish to be caught on that hook. He did a bit more angling on his own account. 'What was the general impression of Chantry?'

MacGregor stifled a sigh. Oh God, they weren't in for another bout of the psychological approach, were they? He tried to remember what had been on the telly recently. If there'd been a repeat of that Maigret series, they were sunk. After a lifetime of wielding his fists to get results, Dover had been intrigued by the idea that some detectives (albeit fictional ones) solved their cases by just sitting and thinking. For a time he had actually adopted the technique – or a slight variation of it. He did away with the thinking bit.

'Cat got your tongue, laddie?'

MacGregor tried to collect his wandering thoughts. 'Sir?'

'I asked you if you'd dug up any motive for Chantry's murder. You got cloth ears or something?'

Motive? MacGregor winced. It was such an unprofessional approach. Means and opportunity – that's what a proper detective should be concerning himself with at this stage. Only when you'd established those did you start looking round for motives. Trust Dover to began at the end and work backwards.

82

'Nothing in particular, sir,' said MacGregor, endeavouring not to sound too disdainful. 'I was more interested in finding out who, in a time-and-space context, could have done the killing.'

Dover rolled his eyes eloquently up towards the ceiling.

'However,' – MacGregor went on – 'I did gather that he wasn't any too popular. He was rather a pushing sort of man and a bit too keen on ramming his views on morality down other people's throats. Still, I would guess he was a man more disliked than actually hated. Did you come across any strong motive, sir?'

Dover was saved by the dinner gong from the effort of answering that one. He swung himself off the bed. 'Grub up, laddie!' he said and wallowed joyfully in MacGregor's evident disappointment. That'd teach the cocky young pup that some people weren't so green as they were cabbage looking!

Six

Dover was alone when he presented himself at the front door
of the Studio and rang the bell. MacGregor, his curiosity having been fanned to obsessive proportions, had been despatched
to the Hoopers to rearrange the time of their interview with
Dover. Only when this mission had been accomplished was he
to be permitted to occupy a ringside seat at the dramatic confrontation which – or so Dover seemed to hint – was to come.

Not that the earlier part of the evening had been deficient in
drama. Dover's appearance in the dining-room had acted like
a red rag to a bull where Mrs Boyle was concerned. Nostrils
flaring, she had launched herself into the attack while everybody else sat around in a cringing and embarrassed silence.
Although Mrs Boyle frequently boasted that she feared neither
man nor beast, she wasn't quite prepared to risk a head-on
collision with Dover. She opted for an oblique assault and in
a loud voice addressed her remarks ostensibly to poor Miss
Dewar.

'One appreciates,' she began, 'the limitations of the male
bladder but that, in my opinion, is no excuse for well-nigh
hourly excursions throughout the entire night.'

The male bladder! Miss Dewar died a thousand deaths.

'Most of us here,' continued Mrs Boyle, carefully avoiding looking at her prey, 'need our rest. We are beyond the age when we can tolerate havin' our sleep shattered by the thoughtlessness of others. You would think that some people, especially in view of their supposedly responsible official positions, would show more consideration.'

The loaded fork in Dover's hand wobbled as the implications of Mrs Boyle's one-sided conversation began to sink in.

'Servants of the public, indeed!' sneered Mrs Boyle. 'It would never have been permitted in my father's day, that I can tell you. He believed in keepin' the artisan classes in the positions to which it had pleased God to call them. I may have told you, dear, about the occasion when he refused to share a railway compartment with some jumped-up little bank clerk who'd had the insolence to buy himself a first-class ticket. My late husband, the admiral, was forced to be more broadminded, of course, but even he knew where to draw the line.'

'That cistern is very noisy,' said Miss Kettering with a temerity that astonished even her.

Mrs Boyle administered a *coup de grâce*. 'That cistern is perfectly quiet,' she thundered, 'if it is not used. I am surprised at you, Miss Ketterin', taking such an attitude. It is that sort of thinkin' that has brought this country to the sorry pass in which we find it today. The mechanics of this hotel's sanitary arrangements have nothin' at all to do with the problem under discussion. They have been with us for a long time and, in spite of repeated complaints to the management, will no doubt be with us for many years to come. It is the selfish and thoughtless use of those facilities which is causin' all the trouble.'

Dover leaned across the table and tapped MacGregor on the arm with his knife. 'If I wasn't a gentleman,' he hissed, 'I'd give that old cow over there a punch up the bracket!'

'And it is not only the flushin' of the cistern, as I am sure you will agree, Miss Dewar,' continued Mrs Boyle, smiling grimly now that she had drawn blood. 'There is also the heavy trampin' up and down the stairs – to say nothin' of the continual slammin' of doors.'

'Some people have . . . difficulties,' ventured Miss Kettering.

'As a married woman, Miss Ketterin',' – came the stern rejoinder – 'I am well aware of that. The late admiral's bowels were a source of great concern to us both, especially towards the end of his life. But, whatever the discomfort, we would never have dreamed of inflictin' it upon other people.'

'Did you hear that?' demanded Dover hoarsely, leaving another smear of gravy on MacGregor's sleeve. 'Talking like that when people are eating! It's downright disgusting.'

MacGregor was by now too full for words. In any case he was trying to block out the whole terrible scene by selecting the eight gramophone records he would take with him on a desert island, should he ever be lucky enough to be cast away on one.

'Continence!' boomed Mrs Boyle. 'Continence and a modicum of self-restraint! I don't think that's too much to ask, do you, Miss Dewar? If it is,' – she gave a very unpleasant laugh – 'we shall have to try some kind of a deterrent.'

'So help me,' swore Dover passionately, 'I'll get that fat bitch if it's the last thing I do!' He glared at MacGregor's barely touched plate. 'Get a move on, can't you? I'm not going to sit here all night and be insulted!'

Back at Mrs Boyle's table Miss Kettering was rallying again. 'What happened to that article you were going to lend?' she asked sweetly.

'The chamber pot?' Mrs Boyle, whatever her faults, was not mealy mouthed. 'Unfortunately I have mislaid the keys to my leather trunk. In any case, I doubt if it would be a solution. You can take a horse to the water,' she proclaimed sententiously, 'but you can't make it drink. But you have no need to worry, Miss Ketterin'. I have other plans. I have issued my final warnin'. Those who choose to ignore it do so at their peril!'

It was at this point that Dover had choked down his last mouthful of crème caramel and stormed out of the dining-room. For a man who was not unused to public abuse, he had put up a very poor show. He had let that opinionated old battle-axe trample all over him without so much as bloodying her nose for her. He must be losing his grip. In a crisis of self-confidence Dover was never one to blame himself. He looked around for a whipping-boy – and there, on cue, was Mac-Gregor slinking after him through the dining-room door.

Not that bawling out MacGregor was much consolation and its effect on Mrs Boyle was negligible. So, as Dover stood on the Studio doorstep waiting for his ring to be answered, he tried to work out something in the way of revenge. Mrs Boyle had to be chopped down to a more manageable size. It would be nice, as he'd thought before, to get the old harridan at least arrested for the murder of Walter Chantry but Dover doubted if even he could manage that.

He pouted sulkily at the Studio door. They were taking their blooming time, and no mistake. He rang again and added a couple of kicks for good measure. The toe of his boot didn't do the sparkling white paintwork much good but it did achieve the required result.

The door opened and a big, bearded man dressed in a shortie flannel nightshirt appeared in the opening. His legs and feet were bare. Dover cheered up. It looked as though the bit about nudism was true anyway.

' You waiting for a tram, Sam?'

Dover tore his eyes away from the big man's toenails. Were they really varnished alternately green and gold? ' Detective Chief Inspector Dover,' he announced with an ingratiating smile, ' from Scotland Yard.'

' Got a warrant?'

' A warrant?' yelled Dover. ' What do I want a warrant for? I only want to ask you a few questions.'

' Is that so?' The big man propped himself up against the door jamb. ' OK, ask away!'

' Out here?'

' Why not? I'm easy. No law, is there, that says we've got to have you inside?'

' No, there's no law,' admitted Dover unhappily, ' but it is usual.'

' So you'll enjoy the change,' said the big man coolly. ' Besides, we've already had one scuffer trampling all over the Aubusson this morning. What gives – a harassment?'

' Murder's a very serious business,' Dover pointed out, shifting his weight from one aching foot to the other.

' Would you believe I save my worrying for ingrowing toenails? What's the matter anyhow – don't parking offences give you a kick any more?'

' What's your name?' demanded Dover, fighting hard not to lose his temper and ruin everything.

' Lloyd Thomas, O shining one! But you can call me master.'

Dover clutched at the straw with a quick wittedness that threats to his personal comfort sometimes inspired. ' Then you're not the householder, are you?'

' Negative,' agreed the big man. ' That's James-Love-Your-Local-Policeman Oliver.' He pushed himself off the door jamb. ' So enter in! Oliver's got foam rubber for a heart. He wouldn't keep even the wolf standing out in the cold.'

Lloyd Thomas padded softly up the stairs and led Dover into a large room on the first floor. Here was assembled as varied a collection of dust-covered junk as Dover had seen in many a long year. Every fad and fashion of the last decade seemed to have made its tawdry contribution. Victoriana fought it out with Art Noveau. African devil masks leered at crumpled examples of Japanese calligraphy. The walls were covered with posters of wanted bad men of the American West, bull fighting and Toulouse-Lautrec, all mixed in with domestically produced graffiti.

Dover searched amongst the bamboo and the stripped pine and the cubes covered in red leatherette for something on which he could sit without doing himself a mischief. That rocking horse in the corner?

Lloyd Thomas felt he had done his share of the honours. 'Wittgenstein,' he said, 'look what I found on the doorstep.'

A young woman, who had been lying sprawled on the floor in front of the stove, sat up, parted the streaky blonde curtain of her hair and looked out. 'Oh, *God*!' she groaned. 'Jim'll go spare! He ordered a strong bone structure, not a bag of jelly.'

Lloyd Thomas folded himself up into the window seat. 'It isn't a model, you idiot! It's a rozzer.'

Dover lowered himself gingerly on to one of the cubes and hoped for the best.

The young woman flopped back on her hearth rug. 'Thank God for that!' she said. 'I couldn't face another of Jim's temper tantrums, not tonight.' She sat up again with a jerk. 'For Christ's sake, not another bloody policeman!'

'Precisely my own sentiments,' said Lloyd Thomas, nodding his head. 'No need to take up panic stations though. It's only about the Chantry murder.'

'Nothing became that man's life like his leaving it,' Miss Wittgenstein commented petulantly. 'A bloody nuisance, quick or dead.'

Dover judged it was about time he started getting in on the act. He settled his feet firmly on a home-made mat decorated with three feathers and the legend 'God Bless Our Prince of Wales' and addressed himself to Miss Wittgenstein. 'You didn't go much on Mr Chantry, eh?'

'Watch it, Wittgenstein!' advised Lloyd Thomas from the window seat. 'Twenty years in Holloway will dull that dewy bloom on your cheeks – and just ruin your development as an artist.'

'Nonsense!' scoffed Miss Wittgenstein. 'I'd never get twenty years, not for a creep like Chantry.'

'They won't give you no illuminated scroll, girlie.'

Miss Wittgenstein reached for a cigarette and lit it by holding it against the red-hot side of the stove. 'Anyhow, who says it's me they're gunning for? I should have thought you two boys were much more alluring suspects.' She caught Dover's appealing glance. 'Want a fag, fuzz?'

'I wouldn't say no,' simpered Dover.

Miss Wittgenstein took the cigarette from her mouth and handed it over, lipstick-decorated end and all. Then she lit herself another.

'Is that wise, Wittgenstein?' asked Lloyd Thomas who had been watching the transaction with some apprehension.

'Wise?' Miss Wittgenstein looked blank for a moment. 'Oh, I see what you mean. Give me some credit, duckie. I'm dispensing tobacco, not tea.'

The mention of the cup that cheers reminded Dover of the main purpose of his visit. 'I could just do with a cup of tea,' he remarked chattily. 'It's thirsty work, asking questions.'

'You've only asked one so far,' said Miss Wittgenstein with a preciseness that Dover could well have done without.

'I haven't started yet!' he retorted with a flash of the old fire. 'Still,' – remembering that fires can burn your boats irretrievably – 'I wouldn't want to put you to any trouble, miss. A glass of beer or such-like'd do me just as well.'

Before Miss Wittgenstein had a chance to pick up this delicate cue, the front door bell rang.

Lloyd Thomas folded his arms across his chest. 'Enough is too much,' he said firmly. 'An Englishman's home is his castle. I propose and second that we raise the jolly old drawbridge.'

The bell rang again.

Miss Wittgenstein rolled over on to her stomach. 'It'll only disturb Jim.'

'Bugger Jim,' said Lloyd Thomas indifferently. 'Just because he's got himself hooked on a working jag is no reason for me to make like a footman, is it?'

'Butlers answer doors,' Miss Wittgenstein pointed out with kindly superiority. 'If you weren't a pig-headed Taffy from up the bloody valleys, you'd know that.'

'Stuff you!' came the amiable reply.

'If it was you, Jim would.'

'Well, it isn't and I'm not. And if you've got dear Jamie's interests so much at heart, why don't you go and answer the bloody door yourself?'

'All right,' said Miss Wittgenstein belligerently, 'I will!' She uncoiled herself like a cat and stood up. 'Oh, God!' She fished despondently down the neck of her blouse. 'Something's gone bust!'

Miss Wittgenstein was dramatically well endowed in certain spheres and Lloyd Thomas was still groping frantically for some suitably bitchy *bon mot* when the door opened and the third member of the household ushered MacGregor in.

From then on things began to move at a more business-like pace. Jim Oliver might have been an artist but he believed in keeping his feet on the ground. Within a matter of moments he had taken control. Dover, as guest of honour, was ceremoniously ensconced in a comfortable chair which had earlier escaped even his eagle eye and a packet of cigarettes was placed conveniently at his elbow. Miss Wittgenstein was despatched to the cellar for supplies of liquid refreshment and Lloyd Thomas was quietly told to go and put his trousers on. Jim Oliver had no more love for the police than his companions had but he knew, from past experience, that rubbing them up the wrong way only ended in tears.

MacGregor found himself a little table and got out his notebook. Jim Oliver, determined to miss out on nothing, sped across with a bunch of newly sharpened pencils.

'So much better than those nasty ball points, dear,' he whispered. 'They never seem to allow you to express your personality, do they? Ah,' – Miss Wittgenstein staggered in with an armful of bottles – 'here comes the plonk! You'll take a glass, won't you, dear? You'll find it astonishingly palatable. What I call a real vintage Algerian.'

MacGregor declined. 'I am on duty, sir.'

Jim Oliver pouted his disappointment. 'Does that mean your delightful chief inspector won't be able to imbibe either?'

Dover had already got both paws round a bottle.

MacGregor hung a sour little smile over his disapproval. 'He's rather a law unto himself,' he said.

'Of course, of course,' cooed Jim Oliver understandingly and took up a dominating position on the hearthrug. 'Now, are you all sitting comfortably? Good, then I'll begin.'

This attempt at the humorous approach didn't go down too well. MacGregor maintained a poker face while Miss Wittgenstein and Lloyd Thomas realistically mimed being sick in a bucket. Dover, needless to say, wasn't even listening.

Jim Oliver gave a nervous cough and turned to MacGregor. 'Well, what is it you want, precisely?'

MacGregor turned to Dover. 'Sir?'

The question was so sharp that Dover jumped and nearly spilled his wine. 'Eh?'

'We're waiting to begin, sir.'

'Oh?' Dover squinted round the assembled company in some bewilderment. As far as he was concerned, they *had* begun. He clutched his glass. He'd got all he'd come for, anyhow.

MacGregor, through tight lips, broke the ignominious silence. 'Shall I carry on, sir?'

Dover scowled at his sergeant and ungraciously nodded his head. 'You do that, laddie.'

The story was pretty much the same as the ones Dover and MacGregor had been listening to all day, except that Oliver, Wittgenstein and Lloyd Thomas, as befitted their status as dissolute artists, were not in bed when the earthquake struck.

'We were in this very room, dear,' explained Oliver, 'and suddenly everything just quivered. Not one of us so much as squeaked. Wasn't that brave? Then we heard this sound of tearing and crashing. It seemed to come from all round. Not particularly loud, really, but ominous. It was old L.T. here who was the first to guess what it was. Well, we all came to the conclusion that we'd be safer outside so we grabbed a few coats and torches and things and headed for the open air.'

'Now, you actually saw Mr Chantry, didn't you?' asked MacGregor with a meaningful – and completely wasted – glance at Dover.

'You must be psychic!' sneered Lloyd Thomas. 'We told you all this this morning. And we didn't so much see as hear. Like we told you, it was pitch dark.'

'We heard people shouting up in North Street,' explained Jim Oliver quickly. 'Mr Chantry was just pulling Pile out of the wreckage when we arrived. Well,' – he pulled uneasily at his left ear – 'we thought the situation seemed under control and we'd probably be more use giving somebody else a hand, so we pushed off.'

Lloyd Thomas leaned forward impatiently. 'Come off it, Jim. These bluebottles have been nosing round the village all bloody day. Somebody'll have marked our card for sure.' He swung round to MacGregor. 'Look, spook, the honest to God is that none of us would have given Pile a helping hand if we'd tripped over him. And likewise for Chantry.'

'Oh, I wouldn't exactly say that,' bleated Jim Oliver, blowing his nose nervously on a paint rag.

'Why not?' Miss Wittgenstein put her glass down with a bang. 'It's milk and water compared with what you did say before Chantry zipped through the pearly gates. I'm on Taffy's side. Let's shame the devil.'

'Oh, nonsense!' blustered Jim Oliver. 'You're making quite unnecessary mountains, my darlings. We didn't like Chantry and Chantry didn't like us, but that doesn't mean . . .'

'I understand that Mr Chantry was trying to evict you from these premises, sir,' said MacGregor quietly.

Jim Oliver gulped and muttered something about gossipy old women. 'That man didn't know his own mind for two minutes together, sergeant. Yes, he was trying to terminate my lease but I'm sure you know as well as I do that that's easier said than done these days.'

'We had a crafty ace or two up our sleeves,' Miss Wittgenstein chimed in and got a furious look for her pains.

'The fact is, sergeant, that I'm the sitting tenant and, as such, I am immovable.'

'Mr Chantry could have been making life rather unpleasant for you, sir.'

'That creep?' bellowed Lloyd Thomas. 'Take it from me, scuffer, where persecution is concerned, Chantry didn't even know where to begin. For God's sake, look at us! Do we look the sort to be scared by a couple of sanctimonious, morality-spouting bastards like Chantry and old Haemorrhoids? What could they do but talk?'

'I'm sure I don't know, sir,' murmured MacGregor non-committally. He had one or two ideas he intended to investigate in his own good time. 'Perhaps we could continue now with your movements round about the time of the murder? You'd decided not to go to the help of the Piles and Mr Chantry. What happened next?'

'Just a minute!' Dover held up a beefy hand which had in its time arrested the flow of London's traffic.

'You have a question sir?'

'Well, I'm not requesting permission to leave the bloody room!' barked Dover to the delight of Lloyd Thomas and Miss Wittgenstein. 'I want to know why these three layabouts took so long.'

'Took so long about what?' asked Jim Oliver anxiously.

Dover jabbed an accusing finger at him. 'Chantry was in bed – wasn't he? – yet he'd time to get up, get dressed and rescue Pile and the girl before you lot even arrived on the scene. Either he ran like the clappers or you were dragging your feet more than somewhat.'

'Ah,' said Miss Wittgenstein quickly, 'but we'd turned the other way first, you see, down East Street. We didn't know where the real damage was and we only came back up towards North Street when we found the road blocked by the church steeple.' She appealed to her companions. 'That's right, isn't it, chaps?'

The chaps agreed that it was.

'What have you got against Pile?' demanded Dover, abruptly switching the point of his attack just for the hell of it.

'He was Chantry's side-kick and little Sir Echo,' said Lloyd Thomas. 'Who wants more?'

'We'd tried to be friendly,' said Miss Wittgenstein, addressing herself to MacGregor because she thought he had a sympathetic face, 'but, honestly, he used to back away from us as though we were lepers or something so now we don't bother. As a matter of fact, I was all for going and giving a hand that night but Jim and L.T. here wouldn't let me.'

'They'd have spat in your eye, girl,' said Lloyd Thomas bitterly. 'Your trouble is you're a dedicated masochist. Remember what happened the last time you tried to play Little Miss Philanthropy-Incorporated.'

Miss Wittgenstein sighed. 'It was soon after they came here,' she explained. 'You see, I've done quite a bit of work with sub-normal children in my time and it's amazing what you can achieve when you go about it properly. Pile's doing all the wrong things with his daughter. He's forever yacking on about how he's devoted his life to her – you know, the big self-sacrifice kick – but the truth is he just keeps the kid cooped up as though she was some sort of animal. And, if you ask me, she's nothing like as backward as everybody makes out. With a bit of proper training she could probably do . . .' She swung her feet up on to the seat of her chair and hugged her knees resentfully. 'Oh, well, out of the sheer goodness of my heart, I offered to have her over here for an hour or so every now and again and do some pottery with her. Well, it's what she needs – an outside interest and a bit of normal company. Pottery would have been ideal and she would have got a hell of a kick out of it, poor little devil, but you should have heard old Pile when I suggested it. He made me feel like some old tart procuring for a Port Said brothel! That man's got a mind like a sewer. Now, if it had been Pile who'd been murdered, I could have understood it. Compared with him, Chantry was almost human.'

'Yes, well,' said Jim Oliver as Miss Wittgenstein paused for well-earned breath, ' it's Mr Chantry we're interested in at the moment, my love. We don't want to keep the police here all night, do we?'

'Why the hell not?' asked Miss Wittgenstein aggressively. 'At least they break up this dreary *ménage à trois*.'

Lloyd Thomas got up and went to perch himself astride the rocking horse. 'The door's never locked, duckie,' he said. 'And you can bugger off any old time you feel like it.'

'Oh yes, you'd like that, wouldn't you?' Miss Wittgenstein tossed her head angrily.

'Three's none,' observed Lloyd Thomas with infuriating composure. 'Anybody with a drop of sensitivity in their veins would have noticed they were highly redundant weeks and weeks ago.'

Miss Wittgenstein bared her teeth in a snarl. 'That's what you think! If Jim wasn't such a soft-hearted slob, he'd have given you your marching orders before you even came.'

'Children, children!' Jim Oliver flashed a few warning glances around. 'Shall we save the dirty linen for later, eh?'

Miss Wittgenstein, determined to exercise her feminine prerogative, collared the last word. 'The only dirty linen round here,' she snapped, 'is on that great hairy brute!'

MacGregor hastened to call the meeting to order before Dover began getting nasty and the three artists were persuaded to continue with their story. To give him his due, Dover was not exhibiting any of his usual signs of impatience. He had, after all, achieved his nirvana: a comfortable chair, free booze and fags. He asked little more from life and the bickering going on around him wasn't really troublesome because he'd stopped listening some time ago. He roused himself now only to empty the last of the wine from his bottle into his glass.

'Well, there's really not much more to tell you, dear,' said Jim Oliver, taking up the tale once more. 'In the darkness we passed quietly by on the other side and left Chantry and the Piles to it. We went off down to the far end of North Street and then Wittgenstein found this boy staggering about with blood pouring down his head. She brought him back here to the Studio to try and fix him up and a few minutes later I came back to get a spade. The Piles were still out in the road talking to Lickes and his wife. Then, Colin Hooper appeared and said that all hell was let out round the Sally Gate and could somebody go along there and give them a hand. Well, I said it wasn't too choice at the far end of North Street, either, and that I was going back there.'

'Did Colin Hooper mention his father-in-law?' asked Mac-Gregor.

'I think so. To tell you the truth, I can't honestly remember but I certainly assumed that Chantry and Hooper had been working together. I must admit I wasn't paying much attention. I was in too big a hurry to get back to Lloyd Thomas with my spade.'

'And you and Mr Lloyd Thomas spent the rest of the night in each other's company?'

'Well, not every minute, of course.' Jim Oliver threw his hands up in a gesture of despair. 'Good heavens, you don't seem to appreciate what it was like! Buildings were falling down and people were lying injured and trapped all over the place. L.T. and I were like everybody else – we were just rushing around doing what we could. It was all pretty chaotic. After a bit Wing Commander Pile turned up and tried to start throwing his weight around but nobody took much notice. Well, with somebody screaming in pain a couple of yards away, you don't break off for a staff meeting, do you?'

MacGregor sighed. 'Were either of you in the Sally Gate area of North Street at all?'

Both men emphatically shook their heads.

'We were up at the other end,' said Lloyd Thomas. 'There was more than enough to keep us busy there, believe you me. I never got nearer to the Sally Gate all night than this house – and that was only when I was bringing people along here for Wittgenstein to minister to.'

MacGregor scratched aimlessly in his notebook. This case was developing into a real stinker, and no mistake. Nobody would admit to more than the vaguest idea of where they were or at what time. Whoever had murdered Walter Chantry was hiding in a most effective smoke-screen of general, and genuine, uncertainty. Damn it all, how could you be expected to solve a murder when you couldn't lay your hands on the slightest shred of evidence? For once, thought MacGregor with a kind of warped charity, they were going to have a failure for which Dover's blundering incompetence couldn't be held entirely responsible.

He collected his wandering thoughts and addressed himself to Miss Wittgenstein. 'Did you see Mr Chantry again, miss?'

Of course she hadn't. 'It was us having those oil lamps that did it, you see,' she said as Jim Oliver officiously opened another bottle of wine for Dover. 'I lit them before I started to patch up this boy we'd found. Before I knew what was happening I'd everybody swarming in like moths round a candle. Scutari wasn't in it! We'd the homeless and injured three deep in the kitchen. Some of the women gave me a hand with bandaging people up and things but, really, most of the time I was just run right off my feet. Chantry may have come in but, if he did, I didn't notice him – and he wasn't the sort of man who'd lurk modestly in a corner. Have you asked any of the others who were here if they saw him?'

MacGregor nodded. He had, and they hadn't.

Dover belched loudly and then, with diminishing enthusiasm, poured himself out another glass of wine. 'Not much kick in this stuff, is there?' he asked, screwing up his face in an expression of distaste.

'Well, no,' admitted Jim Oliver apologetically, 'but then it's not really supposed to . . .'

'Not gone off, has it?' said Dover, sniffing suspiciously.

'Off? Oh, no, I don't think so.'

'Well, you could have fooled me!' Dover forced another tumblerful down his gullet, thought for a moment and then dragged himself to his feet. 'Tastes like bloody vinegar!' he muttered crossly. 'And it goes right through you! Where's the lavvy?'

'The . . .? Oh,' – Jim Oliver leapt forward to open the sitting-room door – 'the first on the left, chief inspector, dear. The light switch is outside on the landing.'

Dover grunted and lumbered out, leaving an uneasy silence in his wake.

Jim Oliver went across and examined the dregs remaining in Dover's second bottle. 'I think this is all right, really, don't you?'

'Depends,' said Lloyd Thomas pointedly, 'how much you drink.'

Seven

To Dover the bathroom appeared as a haven of peace and he settled down there for a well-earned rest, staring blankly at nothing in particular. The evening had turned sour on him. Almost as sour, he reflected, as that blooming red ink they'd had the cheek to give him to drink. If that didn't rot his guts for good and all, he'd like to know what would. He ran his tongue round his mouth. Left his dentures all furry, too! Drunken orgies! That fool, Pile, wanted his brains seeing to, building up people's expectations like that.

After a while Dover found it was getting chilly, just sitting there. He got up with a sigh, adjusted his clothing and wandered disconsolately over to the wash basin. A prolonged examination of his tongue in the mirror did nothing to raise his spirit. True, it didn't look any more unsavoury than usual but that wasn't much consolation. He'd still got a deuced funny taste in his mouth. Maybe, if he could . . . He opened the bathroom cupboard and poked around until he found an antiseptic mouthwash. Oh, well, try anything once.

The resultant marriage of cheap Algerian wine and mouthwash was not a success and Dover spat it out disgustedly into the washbowl. 'Strewth! Perhaps, if he cleaned his teeth . . .

Toothbrushes and toothpaste lay conveniently close to hand but Dover was not a complete barbarian. He knew better than to go shoving somebody else's toothbrush into his mouth, thank you very much! Carefully he selected the most upright set of bristles and covered them with a thick layer of paste. Then he removed his top and bottom set, gave them a good scrubbing, rinsed them under the tap and munched them back into place. Ah, that felt better!

Once having started, Dover saw no reason for not going on and he spent the next five minutes desultorily inspecting the contents of all the jars and bottles he could find. The pickings were disappointingly meagre, Dover – as his best friends could have told him – not having much time for deodorants and such-like effeminate cosmetic muck. Soap and water was good enough for him and he couldn't see why it wasn't good enough for everybody else. Thinking of soap reminded him that his own bar could do with replenishing. Unfortunately the tablet on the wash basin was too thin and slimy to be worth the nicking and he began to look around for where they kept their reserve supplies. A pile of cardboard cartons on the window sill looked promising and he strolled across to investigate further. While he was fumbling to get the first lid off, a light flashed on outside and caught his eye. It was coming from the bedroom of the house opposite and, as Dover watched, a young woman came into view and drew the curtains.

Dover got the lid off his box with a jerk. Bloody talcum powder! He dusted himself down and tried again. Now, that house straight across the road – that'd be Chantry's place, wouldn't it? He frowned slightly as he tried to recall the odd snippets of topographical information that had drifted his way since he'd arrived in Sully Martin. The second carton was abandoned and, craning his head, he peered right and left through the window. Signs of earthquake damage in one direction and the village church in the other. Yes, it must be Chantry's house and the young woman was, presumably, Chantry's daughter.

Dover had another look through the window. A good-sized house, well maintained, standing detached in a nicely laid-out garden. You wouldn't get that for fourpence ha'penny! The envy on Dover's podgy features faded and was replaced by a scowl of annoyance. If there was one cause dear to the chief inspector's heart it was Crime Prevention. Not that he wanted to do himself out of a job completely but he would like to see the work load reduced to more reasonable proportions. Like three days a month. He became a little less despondent when he remembered that a burglary at the Chantry house would drop into the lap of the local police and not in his but it still irritated him to see people simply asking with both hands to be done by the first villain that walked by. A kid of two could get into that house. Garden wall to shed roof to that bedroom window in three easy strides.

Dover propped his elbows on the window sill, lowered his chins on to his hands and relapsed into a good brood.

Meanwhile, back in the sitting-room, those matters which should have been Dover's urgent concern had ground to a complete standstill. MacGregor had no more questions to put on his own account and he was damned if he was going to put them on Dover's when the old fool wasn't even there.

'He's taking a long time,' said Jim Oliver, softening the implied criticism with a feeble grin.

MacGregor concentrated on trying to look as though it had nothing to do with him.

'More than likely he's in there sleeping it off,' said Lloyd Thomas who had not taken to Dover.

'Nonsense!' Jim Oliver was determined to nip that sort of seditious talk firmly in the bud. 'He's not had more than the merest *soupçon*.'

'True, blue! If you call the best part of two bottles the merest *soupçon*.'

Miss Wittgenstein returned to her place on the hearthrug.

'Oh, for God's sake,' she begged, 'don't you two start spitting at each other again! The fuzz's got trouble with his waterworks and, if he wants to spend all night in the bog, I'm damned if I can see what business it is of yours.'

'Trouble with his waterworks?' howled Lloyd Thomas, giving vent to a maniac scream of laughter. 'Where on earth did you get that gem from?'

'Oh, drop dead!'

'No, seriously, duckie, I'm interested. Did he tell you?'

'Of course he didn't! If you must know, it was Mrs Lickes from the Blenheim Towers. She was regaling the queue in the grocer's this morning when I was drawing the rations for you ravenous brutes. No sordid detail was spared us and, since I met up with her again in the post office. I had it all twice over. Poor little Millie Hooper looked positively sick.'

MacGregor's faint heart sank. He was used to having Dover's professional incompetence the subject of ribald gossip from one end of the country to the other but if they were now going to have the disgusting old pig's bodily functions bandied about . . .

Miss Wittgenstein was continuing with scant regard for MacGregor's finer feelings. '. . . and pulling the chain all night long. None of the poor old things can get a wink of sleep. Mrs Lickes said she was afraid there'd be the most terrible shindy if he didn't stop it.'

MacGregor's ears glowed a bright pink.

'The whole village is buzzing with it. Well, you know, Mrs Lickes – the biggest mouth this side of the Pennines. Honestly, in the post office, I thought she was going to start drawing diagrams.'

'Of the waterworks?' guffawed Lloyd Thomas.

Miss Wittgenstein began to giggle helplessly. 'Of course not, you grotty tassel from the Celtic fringe! Though I must say that wouldn't have surprised me. No,' – Miss Wittgenstein wiped the tears from her eyes – 'it was just where everybody's room was in relation to the drains!' Having with difficulty got this last sentence out, Miss Wittgenstein gave herself up to uncontrolled mirth, floundering around on her hearthrug.

Jim Oliver glared at her, and at Lloyd Thomas, too. Irresponsible idiots! Why couldn't they restrain themselves until the cops had gone? He tried to distract MacGregor's attention. 'You don't think he could have been taken ill or anything, do you, dear? I should hate to think of him lying dead or unconscious on the bathroom floor while we were just sitting here.'

It was a solution that had not occurred to MacGregor. He couldn't imagine why. In his mind he had disposed of Dover in some very sticky ways but, somehow, he'd never thought of him just . . .

The sitting-room door burst open.

MacGregor's rosy future turned to dust and ashes. 'Oh, there you are, sir!'

'Where did you think I was, moron? Up the bloody Zambesi?' Dover scowled round at the assembled company. What a way to spend your days, eh? Hobnobbing with a scruffy mob like this! Damned good bath and a haircut all round wouldn't come amiss. No wonder their bathroom was stocked with a ton of bloody cosmetics and only one measly bit of soap. He let fly at MacGregor again. 'You finished here?'

'Yes, I think so, sir. If you have, that is.'

'Me?' Dover's eyes popped indignantly. 'This shower were on your list, laddie, not mine. I got all my interviews done before supper.'

'Well, all except the Hoopers, sir,' said MacGregor before he could stop himself.

Dover's fists clenched longingly. One day this pup was going to go too far and Dover would then arise in righteous wrath and pulverize him! For two pins he'd do it now, if it weren't for the sobering restraint imposed by the presence of three hostile witnesses. A more devious revenge must be temporarily wreaked. 'All right, we'll go and see 'em now,' said Dover, forgetting in the passion of the moment that his sergeant didn't regard overtime as a punishment.

Plagued by the niggling suspicion that he'd been outwitted somewhere along the line, Dover was in no mood to put up with any nonsense from Colin Hooper. That harassed-looking young man had barely got the front door open before he found that one of his unexpected callers was halfway down the hall.

'Here,' he protested as he recognized MacGregor, 'I thought you weren't supposed to want to see us until tomorrow?'

'Supposed wrong then, didn't you?' Dover called back over his shoulder.

Colin Hooper hurried after him. 'But it's not more than an hour since the sergeant here called round and said . . .'

Dover had already found the lounge. 'He must have made a mistake. It wouldn't be the first, believe me.'

MacGregor shut the front door with a slam and strode down the hall, breathing heavily. By the time he entered the lounge, Dover had already taken possession of the greater part of the settee in front of the fire and was placidly ignoring Mr Hooper's feeble objections.

Mr Hooper turned sulky. 'Oh, make yourself at home then!' he muttered crossly and flung a reproachful glance at MacGregor.

Dover didn't need any invitation. He was at home, spiritually speaking at any rate. The pink roses on the wallpaper could have come from his own living-room. And so – *mutatis mutandis* – could the floral pattern of the curtains, the cretonne loose covers and the traditional Axminster carpet. None of your artistic trash here, thank God! Why, if Dover had put his mind to it (which he had no intention of doing) he could probably have given you the brand name of every article of furniture in the room. And if nation-wide advertising isn't a proof of fine quality, what is?

'You'll need a bit more coal on that fire,' said Dover, opening his overcoat and removing his bowler hat.

'It's been banked up for the night,' moaned Mr Hooper. 'We were just going to bed.'

'At this time?' Dover, secure in the knowledge that he could eat two of young Hooper for breakfast and not even notice, squinted at the clock on the mantelpiece. ''Strewth, it's only . . .' He squinted again but the shiny old gold dial, the elaborate black numerals and the delicate filigree of the hands combined to defeat him. '. . . early,' he said.

Mr Hooper wrung his hands rather pathetically. 'We've had a pretty rough time of it lately,' he explained, 'what with Millie's father – er – dying like he did and everything. Millie's absolutely worn out. As a matter of fact she's already gone up to bed.'

'Well, you'll just have to fetch her down again, won't you?' Dover managed to convey by his tone that he was falling over backwards in an effort to be reasonable. 'If you nip upstairs now you'll catch her before she's had time to drop off.'

Colin Hooper could hardly believe his ears. 'Fetch her down?' he stammered. 'In her condition? She's six months pregnant, you know, and . . . Oh, hell!' He broke off with a groan as a whistling kettle in the kitchen began to let off steam. 'I'd better go and turn it off, I suppose. I was just going to make Millie a hot drink.'

'Good idea!' beamed Dover who prided himself on being the perfect guest. 'Make it tea and we'll all have a cup. MacGregor, give that fire a poke while Mr Hooper here goes and brews up.' He turned to Colin Hooper whose somewhat slack mouth was opening and shutting with the desperation of a stranded goldfish. 'You can fetch your wife down while it's drawing, can't you? And make it a good strong cup, laddie! I can't abide tea that hasn't got the strength to crawl out of the spout.'

Dover's instructions were eventually executed to his complete satisfaction and a somewhat mixed foursome found themselves settled round the fire. The room was warming up nicely and the tea was black enough to put hair on your chest.

Something, however, still seemed to be lacking and Dover fidgeted about hopefully on his sofa.

Mrs Hooper, saucer-eyed with fright and weariness, nudged her husband who had perched himself protectively on the arm of her chair. 'You should have brought some biscuits, Colin,' she whispered timidly.

He frowned warningly at her. 'They don't want any biscuits,' he whispered back.

Which is where he was wrong.

Mr Hooper flounced out of the room and then in again with mounting exasperation showing in every line of his face. Much to his wife's dismay he had forgotten the best plates and a clean white doily. A whole packet of biscuits – naked, unashamed and sixpence off – was slapped down on the coffee table with the clear implication that those that didn't like it could lump it.

Dover had a hand out before the coffee table had stopped vibrating.

Colin Hooper nerved himself for a bit of plain speaking. 'Have you found my father-in-law's murderer yet?' he demanded.

'Not quite,' said Dover with the air of a cat positively constipated on canary feathers. 'Not quite.'

'But you are making some progress?'

'Some progress,' agreed Dover, implying that he could say much more were his lips not sealed. 'I think I can safely say that one or two bits of the jig-saw puzzle are beginning to drop into place.'

Oh, Christ, thought MacGregor irreverently, what are we playing now – Hercules Bloody Poirot?

Millie Hooper was staring at Dover as though he were some obese and malignant idol that needed placating. 'You've not had much time,' she said.

'True, true. Mind you, I'm not much of a one for sitting back with my feet up and letting the grass grow under 'em.'

'I can see that,' murmured Millie Hooper.

'But it's not all rushing around like a scalded clockwork mouse, you know.' Dover jerked a fat and grimy thumb at MacGregor. 'That's where young hopefuls like him make their big mistake. It's not dust you want to stir up, I tell 'em, it's your brains!' He leaned forward to address Mrs Hooper more intimately. 'I don't mind telling you I've solved more murders just sitting quietly with my eyes closed than you've had hot dinners.'

'Gosh!' said Millie Hooper.

It was left to Colin Hooper to break up what could have blossomed into a beautiful friendship. 'Did you want to ask us something special?'

'Eh?'

'Well, making a special journey to come round here in the middle of the night, without warning, and . . .'

'I've got my reasons,' retorted Dover, managing to appear sly and defiant at the same time. 'Besides, we didn't make a special journey. I've just been having one of my little chats with that crummy bunch of daubers across the street. Most instructive, that was. Call themselves artists? I tell you, scum like that want . . .'

Even Dover noticed that his words were having a remarkable effect upon young Millie Hooper. Her face had not had much colour in it before but now it blanched to a staring white which made her eyes look bigger and rounder than ever. She tried to stifle the groan that rose to her lips by gripping the sleeve of her housecoat with her teeth.

Colin Hooper turned in alarm. 'Millie, love, what is it?'

She shook her head, unable to answer.

Her distress was catching and it was Colin Hooper's turn to go pale. 'Oh, God,' he cried, 'it's not starting already, is it?' He jumped to his feet and tried to make Millie lie back in the chair. 'Now, just you stay there, love, and don't worry about anything. You'll be all right. Just try and relax, eh? I'll phone for the doctor right away.'

She summoned up enough strength to stop him before he

dashed out of the room. 'No, Colin, I don't need the doctor. It's not that.'

'Well, what is it, love?'

Millie Hooper closed her eyes and then, helplessly, began to sob.

Her husband dropped on his knees beside her, murmuring vague reassurances. When these didn't seem to be doing much good he broke off and rounded angrily on Dover. 'This is all your fault, blast your eyes! Coming round here and frightening the life out of her! Well, I'm warning you, if anything happens to Millie or the baby, I'll kill you, by God I will!'

Dover helped himself to another biscuit. 'You want to watch that temper of yours, laddie. It'll be getting you into trouble one of these days – if it hasn't already.'

'You stinking, sadistic old windbag!' shouted Colin Hooper, losing control and beating his fists on the arm of Millie's chair, 'You've got thirty seconds to get out of my house!'

Millie Hooper, the tears still dribbling down her face, grabbed her husband's hands. 'Oh, Colin, don't!' she begged. 'It's no good. Can't you see. He knows.'

Colin Hooper stared at her. 'He knows?'

'Why else should he come straight round here. She must have told him.'

Colin Hooper's shoulders sagged dejectedly. 'But you said she promised.'

'I know, and she did, pet, but that was before Dad was murdered, wasn't it? Things are different now. You can't blame her really. They probably kept on and on at her until they broke her down.'

'Yes,' agreed Colin Hooper grimly, glaring at Dover, 'bullying women, I should think that's just about their mark.' He put his arms round his wife's shoulders.

Dover passed his empty tea cup to MacGregor for a refill and sat back, quite content to wait until somebody got around to explaining to him what the hell was going on.

'Did she tell you?'

Dover looked Colin Hooper straight in the eye. 'Yes,' he said.

There was a sharp and incredulous intake of breath from MacGregor but Colin Hooper didn't notice. He was too busy putting on a bold face. 'Well, I can't see that it's anything to make a fuss about, not these days. I mean, that Wittgenstein woman's not all that much room to talk, has she? Some of the things they get up to over there'd make your hair curl but nobody goes round pointing a finger at them, do they?'

'My dad did,' sniffed Millie Hooper.

'Oh, yes,' – Colin Hooper nodded his head miserably – 'your dad did.'

'Well, that's what we were bothered about, isn't it? My dad.' She turned apologetically to Dover. 'I don't know what I'm being such a silly about. It's just that I haven't really taken it in yet that my dad's dead.'

'Ah,' said Dover.

MacGregor, as usual, was quicker on the uptake. He had to be, otherwise they'd have been sitting there all night. 'Well, now, madam,' he began with only a hint of menace in his voice, 'perhaps you'd like to give us your version of what – er – happened. We've got Miss Wittgenstein's statement, of course, but we want to be fair and ' – he made a great show of getting his notebook out – 'hear your side of the story.'

'That's right,' agreed Dover quickly so that Mr and Mrs Hooper wouldn't start getting any erroneous ideas about who was top dog. 'You just tell us all about it in your own words.' He gave MacGregor a warning glower. 'Anything that's not clear, I'll ask the questions about.'

Millie Hooper sighed heavily, wiped her eyes on her husband's handkerchief and blew her nose.

'Just a minute!' interposed Colin Hooper, finally dropping to below zero on Dover's popularity chart. 'I don't see what this has got to do with anything.'

'You wouldn't!' snarled Dover. 'Well, take my word for it, laddie, it has.'

'With Mr Chantry's murder?'

'Oh, stop arguing, Colin love,' said Millie Hooper. 'Just let's get it over and done with.' She took a deep breath. 'Colin and me anticipated our marriage vows.'

''Strewth!' groaned Dover and buried his head in his hands.

Millie Hooper felt cheated. When one has bared one's innermost shame to a couple of complete strangers, one at least expects them to be shocked. 'Twice!' she added. 'He climbed up on to the shed and through my bedroom window.'

'And the Wittgenstein woman spotted him from their bathroom,' said Dover, suddenly seeing the light and putting one smartly over MacGregor.

'Yes. Both times.'

'That'll learn you!' sniggered Dover.

MacGregor brought the conversation back to a more elevated level. 'How did you find out that Miss Wittgenstein had seen you? Did she tell you?'

'She couldn't wait,' said Millie Hooper sullenly.

'But she promised not to say anything?'

'She knew my dad would have gone through the roof if he'd found out.'

Millie Hooper was looking decidedly shifty and MacGregor began to probe deeper. 'Did she try to make a bargain with you?'

'A bargain? I'd call it more like blackmail. I don't suppose she told you that bit, did she?'

'Not exactly,' said MacGregor cautiously.

'Trust her!'

'Did she want money?'

Millie Hooper shook her head. 'Where would I have got money from? My dad paid all the bills and everybody in Sully Martin knew I only got two pounds a week allowance. You can't get blood out of a stone. No, she just wanted me to use my influence, that's all.'

'With your father?'

'That's right. All this happened just about the time he started trying to get them tipped out of the Studio. Miss Wittgenstein promised she wouldn't say a word about Colin if I'd persuade my dad to leave them alone. The Studio suited them down to the ground, you see, and they didn't want to leave, especially when the rent was so low.'

MacGregor tapped his pencil thoughtfully against his teeth. 'And you agreed?'

'I hadn't much choice. If my dad had ever suspected . . . I thought it would stall things off until after Colin and me were married because, of course, I daren't say anything to my dad about the Studio. He wouldn't have taken a blind bit of notice if I had.'

'And this satisfied Miss Wittgenstein?'

'Well, they haven't been evicted yet and I kept telling her I was doing my best. To do her justice, I don't think she wanted to tell my dad and, anyhow, there was no proof that he'd have believed her if she had.'

'Hm.' MacGregor made a few aimless squiggles in his note-book to give himself time to think.

Colin Hooper watched him anxiously. 'But, it's like I said, isn't it?' he demanded. 'This has nothing to do with Mr Chantry's murder. I mean, if Millie and me had wanted to do anything, we'd have murdered Miss Wittgenstein, wouldn't we?' The embarrassed laugh which accompanied this supposition fell on particularly stony ground.

'Look, laddie,' said Dover heavily as he hoisted himself up into a better position for bullying, 'from the way things are developing round here, your father-in-law wouldn't have needed the Wittgenstein woman to spill the beans, would he? He'd have guessed for himself that there'd been more than a bit of pre-marital hanky-panky.'

Colin Hooper bit his lip. 'I don't know what you mean.'

'I mean the bun in the oven!' growled Dover. 'What were you reckoning on doing? Passing it off as premature?'

'There was a sporting chance,' muttered Colin Hooper, exchanging an agonized glance with his wife.

'With half the village wearing out their fingertips counting now?' jeered Dover. 'If that kid arrives nine months after your wedding day, it'll have boots on! Now, you listen to me, laddie, because I'm going to give you some good advice. You give us a full confession and I'll put in a good word for you with the judge. Now, I can't say fairer than that, can I?'

'A confession?' Colin Hooper didn't know whether to laugh or cry. He glanced at MacGregor for some sort of guidance but the sergeant's poker face was deliberately set on registering nothing. 'I must be going mad!'

'Oh, I don't know that I'd try that for a defence,' said Dover, graciously giving the matter his careful consideration. 'Suit yourself, of course, but – me – I'd sooner pay my debt to society in a prison rather than a looney bin.'

Colin Hooper clutched his head. 'You can't be serious!'

'A clean breast now'll make things much easier in the long run,' Dover pointed out, without specifying whose convenience he had in mind.

'You mean you're really just sitting there, calmly asking me to put my head in a noose?'

'Ah!' Dover was glad of the opportunity to put this little misconception right. 'That's where you're making your mistake, isn't it? There aren't any of the old necktie parties these days, laddie. More's the pity, of course, but let's look at things from your point of view. I reckon you'd be out in fifteen years or so with the best part of your life still before you. You're one of the lucky ones. A few years ago and you'd have got the drop and no argument. And you don't want to believe all that rubbish you read in the newspapers, either. Quick and painless?' Dover's flabby torso wobbled as he chuckled good-humouredly to himself. 'Not on your nelly! Well, hangmen are only human, aren't they? They make mistakes like the rest of us. It's all a question of judging the drop properly, you see. Underestimate and you're swinging about for hours, slowly choking to death. Overestimate and you get your head torn clean off. Here,' he pulled his feet sharply out of range – 'she's not going to be sick, is she?'

Millie Hooper eventually recovered enough to assure her husband that she was all right, really, and Dover, retreating to the far end of his sofa as a precaution, prepared to continue.

Colin Hooper, however, had had enough. Heaven knows what more of Dover's social chit-chat might do to his unborn child. 'Look, sir, could we get one thing quite straight. There's absolutely no question of my making a confession because I damned well haven't done anything.'

'Come off it!' scoffed Dover. 'You and your missus have got enough motive for a dozen murders.'

'You leave my wife out of this!'

'All right, all right!' Dover's efforts to be obliging were rather touching. 'If you want to shoulder all the guilt, I'm easy. Actually, it's not a bad line to take. Most judges are right suckers for a whiff of the old chivalry. So – we'll put it your way. *You*'ve got enough motive for a dozen murders. You collect all your father-in-law's money and his business, you get this house to yourself and you forestall him finding out that you got his only daughter in the club before you escorted her down the aisle. What sort of an impression do you think that lot's going to make on a jury, eh? Take it from me, laddie, they'd convict you without even leaving the box.'

MacGregor could have sunk through the floor with the shame of it all. A senior Scotland Yard detective going on like this! It was incredible. MacGregor knew it was incredible because it had happened before and none of his superiors, to whom he had submitted a series of highly confidential reports, had believed one word of them.

Colin Hooper jumped to his feet and installed himself firmly in front of the fire in what he hoped was a dominating position. He had wondered about refusing to say another word until he'd got a solicitor to protect his interests but he realized that such a move would only provide Dover with yet more grist for his mill. It was obvious that, in Dover's book, only the guilty invoked their rights.

Colin Hooper cleared his throat and squared his shoulders. 'Chief Inspector Dover, I did not kill Mr Chantry.'

Dover looked up and yawned.

'And,' – Colin Hooper sternly refused to quail – 'I can prove it. On the night of the earthquake I left the house a few minutes after my father-in-law because I had to make sure that Millie would be all right. Well, when I got outside I couldn't see him anywhere. The people in the cottages nearly opposite us were shouting for help and I started trying to get them out. After quite a little time, Mr Chantry came up. He said he'd got the Piles out of their house. Well, things were pretty hopeless where we were and after a bit Mr Chantry suggested that I should go and see if I could find somebody to give us a hand. That was the last time I saw him. I groped my way back to the top of East Street and came across Wing Commander Pile and Mr Lickes, and Jim Oliver was there, too. I told them what my father-in-law had said and Mr Lickes agreed to come back with me. Wing Commander Pile said something about getting some clothes and joining us later. Well, Mr Lickes and I came back over this way. There was a woman trapped somewhere, I think, and Mr Lickes stopped to get her free but I thought I'd better go on and try and find my father-in-law. I looked around for him for a bit as best I could but I couldn't spot him anywhere. After a while I stopped bothering about him. Well, you can't just step over somebody who's screaming for help, can you? I carried on by myself as best I could and I didn't worry about Mr Chantry because I thought he was doing the same sort of thing quite near by. It was only much later, when it got light and the proper rescue people arrived, that Millie and I began to get a bit worried when he didn't show up.' Colin Hooper folded his arms resolutely across his chest. 'Now, is there anything else you want to know?'

Dover stared disconsolately into as much of the fire as he could see with Colin Hooper's legs in the way.

MacGregor, however, had a few questions. 'You say you were working in the area over towards the Sally Gate?'

'That's right.'

'That's in the vicinity of where Mr Chantry's body was found?'

'Yes.'

'And you still claim that you didn't see him?'

'It was dark, sergeant, and raining quite heavily. Most of the time I was groping and crawling around up to my waist in mud. Mr Lickes was around somewhere and I never saw him, either. Frankly, I was too worried about slipping down the hillside myself to bother about what other people were doing.'

'But there were other people about?'

'Yes, but it's no good asking me who they were. They were just vague figures and I simply didn't notice. There were people dead and dying all round me, you know. Well,' – he realized this was a trifle over-dramatic – 'injured, anyhow.'

Dover was turning a distinctly lack-lustre ear to these exchanges. Since he had failed to nail Colin Hooper with one swift blow below the belt, his interest in furthering the cause of truth and justice waned. All, as far as his jaundiced eye could see, was rapidly turning to gall and wormwood. The tea was drunk, the biscuits eaten and even that bloody fire was dying down. The meagre crumbs of the Hoopers' hospitality had been consumed and the red Algerian wine was gnawing sourly at the lining of his stomach. It was time to go.

'Come on!' he said to MacGregor.

MacGregor discarded the craftily phrased question he had just worked out. 'But, sir . . .'

'But, nothing!' Dover extricated himself with a great deal of puffing and blowing from the depths of the sofa and screwed his bowler hat back on his head. While he waited for the stiffness to go out of his legs, he improved the shining hour by delivering a parting broadside in the direction of Colin Hooper.

'You've had your chance, laddie! If you'd played ball with me, I'd have played ball with you. Next time I come knocking at your door there'll be a warrant in my hand. For murder!'

Eight

'Ungrateful bastard!' grumbled Dover.

MacGregor didn't need to ask to whom he was referring. In the short walk from the Hooper residence back to the Blenheim Towers they had already had this conversation three times.

'And you're no better,' continued Dover. 'If you'd joined in instead of sitting there like a stuffed dumb-bell, he'd have cracked soon as look at him. Of course,' he added with a burst of generosity, 'I blame myself. I should have cut the cackle and bloodied his nose for him. That's the only language his sort understand. A couple of good thumps round the ears and he'd have sung like the Luton Girls' Choir.'

'The wife . . .' murmured MacGregor, recognizing his cue.

'I thought we were going to have the brat arriving on the hearthrug as it was. If I'd really started roughing pretty boy up, she'd have gone into labour just to thwart me. Still, I'll get the bastard yet.'

'I'm afraid we haven't got much against him in the way of evidence, sir.'

'I know that, dolt!' snapped Dover. 'If we'd got any bloody

evidence, we wouldn't want a free and voluntary confession, would we? Didn't they teach you anything at this posh school you're supposed to have gone to?'

'Mind you, sir,' said MacGregor meekly, 'he does admit to being in the area where Chantry was killed.'

'So does Lickes.'

'The way I see it, sir,' said MacGregor, adjusting his pace to keep down with Dover's unathletic waddle, 'Mr Chantry must have been killed pretty soon after he rescued Wing Commander Pile. Apart from young Hooper, nobody admits to seeing him after that and I can't help thinking somebody would have spotted him if he'd been around. He strikes me as the kind of fellow who would have made his presence felt, even in the middle of an earthquake.'

Dover was wrapped up in his own speculations. 'Maybe Lickes did it,' he mumbled as they turned into the hotel drive. 'Or Pile. He's got a very shifty look, that fellow.'

'But has he any motive, sir? He doesn't appear to stand to gain in any way from Chantry's death and, by all accounts, they were the very best of friends. And Chantry had just saved his life – or as near as makes no difference.'

'The potty daughter could have done it.'

'Without her father knowing, sir?'

'Well, he'd cover up for her, wouldn't he?'

'I doubt if Miss Pile would be anything like strong enough, sir. I've been checking through the medical reports again. Considerable physical strength was used and, although Chantry wasn't by any means a husky sort of chap, I think he'd have been more than a match for Linda Pile. Manual strangulation, sir – that means she'd have had to have done it with her bare hands.'

Dover plodded up the steps to the front door. 'They have the strength of ten.'

'So I've heard, sir.' MacGregor followed his chief inspector into the pitch-dark hall and wished, as he had often wished before, that Dover wouldn't base all his scientific observations on old wives' tales. 'Oops – I beg your pardon, sir!'

'Why don't you look where you're going?' snarled Dover who had stopped dead in his tracks precisely because he couldn't. 'Where's the light switch?'

Under the cover of darkness MacGregor backed off a foot or two and surreptitiously brushed down his coat. He was inclined to be rather over-fastidious. 'I'm afraid I've no idea, sir.'

'Trust you!' Dover peered around. 'The bloody fools! Somebody might break their neck, groping around in the dark like this. Here,' – he grabbed hold of MacGregor and pushed him forward – 'you go first.'

MacGregor fished his cigarette lighter out and in its flickering light the pair of them shuffled their way gingerly across the hall and up the stairs. Dover, as was only to be expected, made the worst of a bad job and their noisy progress was peppered with heartfelt obscenities as he blundered into walls and furniture.

'Damned morons!' he bellowed as he reached the first-floor landing and he mounted a final stair which wasn't there. 'What do they think they're running, for God's sake? A bloody nunnery?'

MacGregor fumbled hopefully along the wall for the light switch. 'It is getting rather late, sir.'

'Late?' Dover knocked over a chair which should never have been there in the first place. 'Nine o'clock isn't late, even in this superannuated doss house.'

'Actually, sir, it's nearly a quarter past eleven.' MacGregor found the switch and thankfully put the landing light on.

'Rubbish!' muttered Dover, propping himself up against the wall to recover his breath.

'If you'd like to hang on here a second, sir, I'll just run upstairs and switch the light on up there.'

Dover eyed MacGregor suspiciously. 'What the hell are you whispering for?' he demanded.

'I think everybody's in bed asleep, sir.'

This educated guess was only half accurate, in the case of Mrs Boyle. In bed – yes – but no longer asleep. Roused now both to wakefulness and blind fury, she seized the shillelagh which she kept by her bed to repel invaders and began to belabour the wall. The violence of her blows woke up everybody who had not already been disturbed by Dover's return.

MacGregor turned tail and fled upstairs but Dover was made of sterner stuff. 'I'm going to the bathroom first,' he shouted after his retreating sergeant. 'It'll save me coming down those bloody stairs again.'

For the ensuing ten minutes the Blenheim Towers Private Hotel rocked to the cacophony of a hideous duet. As Dover pulled chains, banged seats and slammed doors, Mrs Boyle retaliated with ever more frenzied whacks with the shillelagh. Honours were about even when Dover emerged with a final crash from the bathroom. He was about to indulge in a subtle change of tactics by initiating a short pause in the proceedings. If all went according to plan Mrs Boyle would drop her guard – and her shillelagh – whereupon Dover would take the final and uncarpeted flight of stairs up to his room *con brio*.

An unnatural peace descended as Dover stood motionless in the middle of the landing and held his breath. He'd reckoned on maintaining the cease fire for a good five minutes but boredom set in after the first thirty seconds. He glanced around for something to occupy his bird brain, or even a chair to sit on, and saw that there was a chink of light coming from under the door of Miss Kettering's room. Dover sniggered softly to himself and tiptoed across. Repressing a grunt he bent down and applied his eye to the keyhole. If it hadn't been for his lumbago he would doubtless have been able to assume an upright and innocent stance before Miss Kettering had got her door completely open.

'I thought it was you,' whispered Miss Kettering triumphantly as Dover straightened his back with a wince. 'I could hear your tummy rumbling.' She inclined her head. 'Are you coming in?'

Dover hesitated, not wishing to be compromised by a temptress of such a hoary vintage.

'Oh, come on!' urged Miss Kettering. 'You can't go on patrolling all night without a bit of a break. Besides, I've just treated myself to a box of liqueur chocolates.'

The creak of Dover's boots as he stepped over the threshold proved that Miss Kettering had found the way to the heart of at least one man. Very sensibly she paved the path with no less than three liqueur chocolates and chatted merrily on while Dover let a stream of orange curaçao, kummel and cherry brandy trickle down his gullet.

'I think it's so brave of you, dear, keeping guard on us all through the night. And it's not as though you're a young man, is it? Oh,' – she tapped Dover reassuringly on the arm – 'you needn't look so taken aback! I realize it's meant to be a great secret and I haven't mentioned it to a soul. Well, it was pretty obvious, really – you spending all your days in bed and your nights wandering round the hotel. What else could you be doing? I must confess I did think of telling Mrs Boyle because her attitude is most unreasonable, isn't it? But then I thought it would only alarm her unnecessarily if she found out the truth. Do you honestly think the murderer is going to strike again?'

'Ugh,' said Dover, his dentures cemented together by a wedge of chocolate.

'Have another!' cooed Miss Kettering. 'Take two while you're at it.'

Dover obliged and got drambuie and green chartreuse this time. The combination was fierce and his head gave an involuntary twist.

Miss Kettering, jumping like a gazelle to false conclusions, thought he was looking round her room. 'I'm afraid you must think everywhere's in a terrible mess,' she simpered.

'Oohwaagh!' said Dover and accepted another chocolate to take the taste of the last lot away.

'I call it my little museum of the occult,' twittered Miss

Kettering proudly. 'It may not look like it, you know, but I can lay my hands on anything I want at a moment's notice. My tarot cards, a unique collection of love philtres in those bottles, coffin nails, my astrological charts on the wall, my voodoo drums over there in the corner.' Miss Kettering waved her hands expressively round the room. 'My goodness, you certainly need some equipment these days!'

'Gurawuff!' said Dover, mopping his forehead.

'Have another!' Miss Kettering urged him. 'Go on, dear – force yourself! Now, over there in that other corner,' – she pointed to where the edge of the carpet had been turned back – 'that's where I'm practising my magic circles. Of course, you can't even start summoning devils before midnight but I thought I'd better have a quick run through first. You get absolutely no protection if you make a mistake, you know, and all these signs and things are terribly complicated. Do you like my stuffed raven? I really ought to have a black cat, too, but Mrs Boyle made such a fuss when I barely broached the idea.'

Dover removed his bowler hat so that the air could get to his head and leaned weakly against a table. Miss Kettering, a little disturbed by the way his eyes had suddenly gone a funny red, pushed the box of chocolates at him. Dover focused his eyes and, at the second attempt, made his selection.

'Ah,' said Miss Kettering, getting a mite flustered and moving her ouija board out of harm's way, 'I see you're admiring my dollies.'

'Your dollies?' gasped Dover. He calculated that it was worth jollying the old trout on since the chocolate box was not yet empty.

'Yes. You know, the effigies one makes of one's enemies. I should have thought you would have known about them. I did them quite early on in my correspondence course. Mind you,' – she picked up the plumpest dolly and adjusted one or two of the pins sticking in it – 'there's a lot more to it than just making the models. You need to incorporate a wisp of hair or a few nail clippings for the best results. And then the incantations are most important. It took me simply hours to get this one fixed up.'

Dover looked somewhat sceptically at the plump dolly. 'Does it work?'

Miss Kettering sighed. 'Not as well as the correspondence course people led one to anticipate,' she admitted sadly. 'But I have had one or two minor successes.' She indicated a large pin which had been thrust through the middle of the dolly's left leg. 'She did complain of rheumatism five days after I jabbed that one in.'

Seeing that Miss Kettering's attention was concentrated elsewhere, Dover quietly helped himself to another chocolate. 'She?' he questioned through a bulging mouth.

Miss Kettering giggled and looked suitably shamefaced. 'Can't you guess?' She held the dolly up so that Dover could see it better.

Dover caught a stream of anisette before it dripped right off his chin and examined the dolly more closely. The hair fashioned out of corrugated paper painted silver? The crudely thick ankles? The huge nobbly nose? 'Not Mrs Boyle?'

'Who else?'

Dover looked at the figurine again.

Miss Kettering could read his mind like an open book. She selected a businesslike hatpin from the collection on the table. It had a carved jet bead on the end. 'Would you like to try your luck?'

Dover considered it obligatory to make his position quite clear. 'A load of old codswallop,' he remarked as he accepted the pin.

'Of course, of course, dear!' Miss Kettering pushed the dolly into Dover's hands and trotted off to her bookshelf to find a spell with a really good punch to it.

Dover blew dubiously down his nose. Oh, well, you never knew – and they did say it was the thought that counts. He turned the dolly over, selected a likely looking spot in the area of the lower back and struck.

'That'll make her sit up!' grinned Miss Kettering, coming back with one of the handbooks from her correspondence course. 'Have another . . . Oh, we seem to have eaten them all! What a couple of greedy grunters we are! Do you know, that was a pound box! Oh,' – as Dover began to edge towards the door – 'you're not going, are you? I was hoping you'd give me a hand with the incantations. I suppose duty calls, does it? Oh well, I mustn't detain you but hang on just a sec while I see if I can find you an amulet.' Miss Kettering scurried over to her dressing-table and began hunting through the drawers. Dover, on the off chance that you might be able to eat it, stood upon the order of his going.

'Here we are!' Miss Kettering waved a small brown object about the size and shape of a pill box gaily over her head. 'Now, if I can just find those silly old thongs . . . Got them!' She advanced purposefully on Dover.

'What do you do with it?' he demanded.

'Well, actually you're really supposed to wear it strapped across your forehead. I got it from one of those mail-order firms and there was a picture of an Onondaga Indian Squaw wearing it that way.' Miss Kettering acknowledged that this was unlikely to lure Dover. 'You could keep it in your pocket, I should think,' she went on, 'and I'm sure the smell will go off completely in time.'

Dover was not one for putting himself out for anybody but he showed his gratitude by letting Miss Kettering down gently. 'I reckon I'll go on relying on my strong right arm,' he said modestly.

'Oh well, perhaps you're right.' Miss Kettering dropped the amulet back in the drawer. 'After all, it's all in the mind, isn't it? And you've nothing to worry about.'

'Haven't I?' said Dover.

'I can tell by your aura,' confided Miss Kettering, finally establishing herself as a witch of many parts. 'It's all there. You'll die in your bed all right.'

Dover didn't find this prognostication quite as reassuring as

Miss Kettering doubtless intended it to be but, on the whole, he was feeling pretty pleased with life as he stumped up the stairs to his room. He'd forgotten all about his plan to catch Mrs Boyle napping but he managed it just the same. The row he kicked up brought her with a jolt out of a shallow sleep and for a few seconds she couldn't imagine where she was or what was happening. Then comprehension dawned and, gritting her teeth, she groped for the shillelagh. It was not Mrs Boyle's night and for a long time she couldn't find it. When at last she fished it out from where it had rolled under the bed, she had missed the bus. Dover's second boot had long since walloped into the ceiling immediately over her head.

Mrs Boyle sank impotently back, quivering with rage. Never had she endured such humiliation, not even from the late admiral who had once, early in their married life, tried to assert himself. She set her jaw grimly. One who had successfully cowed the Knave of the Nore in the full flush of his manhood was not going to be beaten by an overblown Bow Street Runner. She began to plot a hideous revenge.

Gradually the minutes tick-tocked away and the Blenheim Towers warily settled down for what was left of the night. Under his eiderdown Dover bubbled and snorted as his digestive juices set about tackling the gastronomic problems his all-embracing greed had set them. From time to time the building itself creaked and groaned and sighed as old buildings will. The sounds were eerie and a nervous person might even have imagined that there was somebody creeping about in the inky darkness.

Half past one struck faintly from the grandfather clock down in the hall. MacGregor muttered ' Gwendoline!' in his sleep, turned over restlessly and settled down again without waking up. It was a dreadful scream, cutting achingly through the silence like a knife through metal, that got him halfway out of his bed before his eyes opened.

The heavy thud which followed the scream passed almost unrecorded as MacGregor flung himself at his bedroom door.

Out on the landing his hand shot automatically to the electric light switch. The staircase flooded into visibility. For a second everything was blurred and he blinked rapidly as he tried to get the still, shapeless mound at the bottom of the flight of stairs into focus.

He'd had more than enough experience to recognize that it was a body, and a dead body at that. He couldn't see the head but the feet trailed limply up the two bottom stairs. He began to hurry down, unable to stifle an unworthy thrill of pure joy. The old fool had got his come-uppance at last! And no one had more richly deserved it! As MacGregor reached the foot of the stairs he became aware that doors were being opened all over the hotel. He caught the confused babbling of anxious voices and quickly wiped the happy smile off his face. The decencies had to be observed.

The body lay ominously motionless. A broken neck, thought MacGregor cheerfully.

'What's happened?' Wing Commander Pile's authoritative voice cut querulously through the babble. His bare feet slapped to a brisk one one-two halt as he caught sight of the body. 'Good God, it's Mrs Boyle!'

'Mrs Boyle?' MacGregor's euphoria fought a valiant rearguard action. 'It can't be!'

Wing Commander Pile mastered his own evident astonishment and glanced sharply at MacGregor. 'Pull yourself together, man!' he barked. 'You've gone as white as a sheet. Of course it's Mrs Boyle. If it isn't, somebody else is wearing her housecoat and her slippers.'

MacGregor sank to his knees beside the body. 'Keep everybody else well back, will you, sir?' he requested in a voice broken with disappointment. Gently he pulled a fold of the flowered housecoat back from the head and his last wild hopes vanished. It was Mrs Boyle all right. He heaved a deep sigh and felt for the heart. One look at the face had been more than enough to confirm his earlier impression but he felt that he had to go through the motions. He was just raising the eyelids when, now neatly arrayed in red leather slippers and a dark blue dressing-gown, Wing Commander Pile returned.

' I've sent the ladies back to their rooms,' he announced in clipped, controlled tones. ' Old Mr Revel is still fast asleep in his bed and I don't see any point in wakening him. Mr Lickes is awaiting my instructions at the top of the stairs. He wants to know if he should telephone for the police and a doctor. He's not quite sure of his responsibilities with you being present.'

MacGregor got slowly to his feet. ' Yes, we shall want the police and a doctor.'

The wing commander marched away and relayed the instructions. He came back to find MacGregor gazing thoughtfully up the stairs. ' She is dead, is she?' he asked.

MacGregor nodded. ' I'm afraid so. From the way she's lying it looks as though she must have fallen down the stairs.'

' Fallen down the stairs?' Wing Commander Pile followed the direction of MacGregor's eyes. 'But, what would she be doing up there in the middle of the night?'

' I've no idea sir,' said MacGregor, trying to shake off the uncanny feeling of indifference and lassitude that had crept over him.

' I suppose we mustn't move her?'

' Good heavens, no!' MacGregor was jerked back to his professional responsibilities. ' The local police will see to all that. And now, sir, if you wouldn't mind, I'd be grateful if you would go to your room and stay there until you're required.'

Wing Commander Pile didn't look best pleased at this request but, after a moment's hesitation, he shrugged his shoulders and withdrew. He went into his daughter's room and, no sooner had the door shut, than MacGregor heard Mr Lickes hurtling up the stairs from the hall. Mindful of possible clues, MacGregor stepped delicately over the body and met the new arrival halfway along the landing.

The police were on their way.

' What else do you want me to do?' asked Mr Lickes, excitedly bouncing about from one side to the other as he tried to get a glimpse of the corpse beyond MacGregor's shielding body.

'Just go back to the hall, sir, and man the telephone, if you will. And when the police come, if you could send them up here straight away.'

'All right.'

'And I'd be obliged, sir, if you would try not to touch or disturb anything as far as you can.'

Mr Lickes stopped bouncing. 'Golly!' he said in an awed voice. 'Here, you don't think this is another murder, do you?'

MacGregor produced the stock, non-committal answer to that question and sped Mr Lickes on his way. Then, quietly and quickly, he checked the first-floor rooms. Everybody was accounted for. Miss Dewar and Miss Kettering clung together like enamoured chimpanzees and informed MacGregor that nothing would tempt them to venture out until the sun stood high in the heavens. Mr Revel was still placidly asleep and Wing Commander Pile was keeping his daughter company in her room. He sat rigidly beside her bed while she contentedly cut coloured pictures out of a magazine.

'Excuse me, sir,' – MacGregor paused in the doorway – 'but I've accounted for everybody except Mrs Lickes. Did you see her by any chance?'

Wing Commander Pile nodded and, crossing over to the door, more or less edged MacGregor back on to the landing. 'Yes, she was with her husband. If you want to find her now, I should try the kitchen. That woman reacts to every crisis by making a pot of tea.'

'No, it doesn't matter, sir, as long as I know she's knocking around. I shall be seeing everybody later, of course.'

MacGregor returned to his dead body and, rather tardily looked at his watch. Damn – he should have checked that earlier! He'd better nip upstairs and get his notebook. When the local police arrived they would expect to find that everything . . .

MacGregor's mouth slowly dropped open. He'd had a niggling sort of sensation for some time that something was missing and now he realized what it was. Where was Detective Chief Inspector Dover? He, a loud-mouthed sufferer from insomnia, couldn't possibly have slept through all . . .

MacGregor leapt over the late Mrs Boyle and raced up the remaining stairs two at a time. Dover's bedroom door was locked. MacGregor hammered on the panels.

Inside the room a waxen-faced Dover removed his head from the blankets which had been sheltering it ever since Mrs Boyle's blood-curdling death scream had rent the night air. 'Who is it?' he asked in a tremulous voice.

'It's me, sir. Sergeant MacGregor. Are you all right, sir?'

Very cautiously Dover got out of bed and pussy-footed over to the door. 'Are you alone?' he whispered.

'Alone, sir? Yes, I'm alone. Why?'

Dover thought about it for a minute or two and then, unlocking the door, grudgingly opened it the merest crack. He squinted suspiciously through at MacGregor, ascertained that the sergeant had been speaking the truth and stood back to let him enter the room. 'What the hell's been going on?' he demanded.

'Well, sir . . .' MacGregor swung round to find that the door had been smartly shut and locked behind him and that Dover was hurrying back to bed with the key in his hand. 'Is anything the matter, sir?'

'Ho,' puffed Dover nastily. 'I was wondering when you were going to ask. If I had to rely on you, I'd be sitting here with my bleeding throat cut.'

'I'm afraid I don't quite understand, sir.'

'Surprise, surprise! There's a murderous attempt on my life and you don't understand.'

'Your life, sir? But it was Mrs Boyle who . . .'

'They were after me!' insisted Dover furiously. 'And wipe that stupid grin off your face! My life's in danger and all you can find to do is sit on your backside and snigger!'

MacGregor took a hold on himself. He'd never had to cope with a persecution mania before. 'I should think it's more than likely that Mrs Boyle just had a heart attack, sir, and fell . . .'

'When I'm interested in what you think, laddie, I'll send you a telegram.'

MacGregor sighed. 'What is it exactly that you want me to do, sir?'

'I want you to get back out there and detect, you bloody fool!' howled Dover. 'What else?'

'But won't you be wanting to direct the investigation yourself, sir?'

'What? And give 'em another chance to get me? Not likely!' He stopped as the sound of footsteps and voices came up from the landing below. 'What's that?'

'I imagine it's the local police arriving, sir. I think I'd better go down and have a word with them.'

Dover relaxed his hold on the edge of his blanket. 'Don't bring 'em up here,' he said. 'I'm not letting anybody in this room until you've got that raving maniac behind bars.'

MacGregor held out his hand. 'If I could have the key, sir?'

Dover scowled resentfully and began to climb out of bed. 'I'll let you out,' he muttered. 'And we'd better arrange a code for when you come back. Two knocks, a pause and then two more. Got it? And if the murderer's got a gun stuck in your back, give six short taps. That way I'll know not to open up.'

Mindful of the fact that they had not exactly shone over the murder of Walter Chantry, the local CID went quite mad over Mrs Boyle. When MacGregor emerged, with some difficulty, from Dover's room it was to find the place swarming with plain-clothes men of every description. Flash bulbs were going off like a tropical storm and the air hung thick with fingerprint powder. MacGregor picked his way carefully through a welter of rubber gloves, plastic bags and foot rules to where a familiar face was beaming over the chaos.

'Good morning, sir.'

'Ah, sergeant!' Superintendent Underbarrow was looking very neat and trim in his uniform. 'Well, you'll have to admit we've done you proud this time, eh? Luckily they've got the main road clear now and I delivered the whole team up here in under twenty minutes. We're setting up the murder head-quarters in the hotel lounge and I'll have a couple of extra phones installed by mid-morning. Meanwhile I've got four motor-cyclists standing by outside for despatch duty and a couple of squad cars.'

'Are you in charge of the operation, sir?'

'Not likely!' chuckled Superintendent Underbarrow. 'That's Detective Inspector Stokes's pigeon. I've just come along to see to the administrative details. He's downstairs start-ing the murder diary so I'll introduce you to him later. Of course, if we find this case is connected with the Chantry busi-ness, we shall place ourselves under your direction. We don't want to have two teams working at cross purposes, do we?'

MacGregor, somewhat stunned by all this feverish activity, watched a plain-clothes man crawling slowly on his hands and knees down the whole length of the landing. 'You don't think you're going to rather a lot of trouble unnecessarily, do you, sir?' he asked guardedly. 'I mean, she was an elderly woman. I should have thought a simple heart attack was probably the most likely explanation.'

Superintendent Underbarrow was having a field day. 'Oh, there's no question of a heart attack, sergeant. The doctor's already given her a preliminary once-over. Subject to con-firmation, of course, she broke her neck.'

'It could still be accidental death, sir,' said MacGregor, finding himself being gently pushed aside by a photographer.

Superintendent Underbarrow postponed shattering the poor lad's illusions on this point while he dealt with a more urgent matter. He leant forward and tapped the photographer on the shoulder. 'How about one for the old family album, eh, Cliff?'

'Sure,' agreed the photographer, amiably winding his film on. 'How do you want it? Arms folded with your foot on her head?'

Superintendent Underbarrow chuckled and excused himself for a minute to MacGregor. 'The missus likes to keep a record, just for the kids,' he confided as he assumed a rather dramatic pose beside the mortal remains of Mrs Boyle.

'Watch the birdie!' said the photographer and fired off half a dozen shots from various angles. 'Right you are, Super! Well, we're finished with the derelict corpse now, if you are. Shall I tell the boys from the meat wagon to come and get it?'

'He's a lad, isn't he?' said Superintendent Underbarrow admiringly as the photographer hurried away. 'But first class at his job,' he added quickly as he caught the look on Mac-Gregor's face. 'Now, where were we? Ah, yes, accidental death. Well, not with that hook screwed in the wall, would you say?'

'Hook, sir?'

'And the wire.' The superintendent had every reason to be highly satisfied with the effect he was producing. 'Didn't you notice them?' he asked innocently.

MacGregor felt himself going pink. 'Well, no, sir,' he admitted.

'Oh, I'll show you, then. I think you'll find it interesting.'

The superintendent cast an eye over the plain-clothes men who were beginning to pack up their equipment. 'Who's got that bit of wire we found? Oh, Fred – give us the loan of it for a few minutes. Ta!' He turned back to MacGregor. 'There you are, sergeant, six foot or so of fine, best quality wire, slightly used. Now,' – he led the way up to the top of the stairs – 'here's the hook, see, screwed firmly down at the bottom here in the wall. Look how shiny it is. It's not been there long, has it? Now, look at this wire. You can see from these bends in it where it's been fastened through this hook and across the width of the stairs and then round the bottom of this upright on the banister. You can see where the wire's cut into the wood.'

MacGregor got down on his hands and knees and examined everything very carefully. He would have been delighted to find something to refute Superintendent Underbarrow's deductions but he couldn't. The shape and length of the wire, the screw itself, the scratches on the screw and the woodwork of the banister could only add up to one thing.

Superintendent Underbarrow had no inhibitions about putting the inevitable conclusion into words. 'Premeditated murder,' he said, and smacked his lips.

Nine

It was several hours later when MacGregor mounted what was now being called the 'Fatal Flight' with Dover's breakfast tray. His passage past the temporary murder headquarters in the lounge had occasioned a few raised eyebrows and a few sniggers but MacGregor prided himself on being big enough to ignore them. One must expect these provincial boys to be a rather crude lot.

He knocked according to the agreed code on Dover's door and, when he was let in, was surprised to find that the chief inspector was partly dressed.

'Are you going out, sir?' he asked as he put the tray down on the dressing table.

Dover carefully locked the door. It was actually the memory of Miss Kettering's prediction that he would die in his bed that had shifted him out of it. A man in as vulnerable a situation as Dover felt himself to be couldn't take too many risks. He responded to MacGregor's damn-fool question with a grunt that might mean anything and dragged a chair up to the dressing table.

MacGregor perched himself on the window-sill and got his notebook out. 'These local chaps have certainly been getting their skates on, sir,' he began chattily as he rifled through the pages. 'Their technique strikes one as a bit – well – unpolished perhaps, but they've certainly got all the basic stuff tied up. I'll fill you in on the groundwork first, shall I, sir?'

Dover had poured himself out a cup of tea and was now occupied with adding sugar by the half pound. He pushed the cup over in MacGregor's direction. 'Try that!' he said.

'I beg your pardon, sir?'

'You want to poke that wax out of your ears, laddie! I told you to have a sip out of that cup.'

'But I've already had my breakfast sir.'

'I don't give a damn if you've had the bloody measles!' retorted Dover impatiently. 'I want you to taste that tea. And the bacon and the eggs and the toast and the butter and the marmalade. Can't you get it into your thick head that somebody's trying to murder me?'

MacGregor was stupefied. 'And you want me to . . .?'

'What else? They could have slipped poison into any of that lot easy as falling off a log. I'm not touching a thing until I know it's safe.'

MacGregor didn't imagine for one moment that Dover's breakfast had been tampered with but he experienced a rather unpleasant tightness in his throat as he duly humoured the old fool by taking a token mouthful of each item of food. Dover watched the proceedings with a gimlet eye.

'Taste anything funny?' he asked.

MacGregor swallowed down a piece of toast. 'No, sir.'

'Hm. Well, we'll wait a couple of minutes and, if you haven't keeled over by then, I reckon I might risk it.'

'Shall I carry on with the briefing meanwhile, sir?'

'You might as well. But, if you start getting any twinges, you let me know right off.'

'Very good, sir.' MacGregor returned to his notebook. 'Well, Mrs Boyle, sir, died just after half past one this morning.'

'And good riddance!' muttered Dover, gazing at his breakfast with longing.

'She died of severe injuries, sir, which included a broken neck and a broken back.'

'Did she, by golly!' Dover, recalling the pin he had stuck in Miss Kettering's dolly, was more than a little impressed. 'It must be a coincidence,' he said uneasily.

'Sir?'

'Oh nothing!' Dover couldn't bear to wait any longer. He grabbed his knife and fork and, after a quick glance at Mac-Gregor to make sure that he was still hale and hearty, started in on the bacon and eggs. 'Well, go on, laddie!'

'The doctor was a little surprised at the extent and severity of Mrs Boyle's injuries but she was, of course, a very heavy old woman and she must have fallen extremely awkwardly. He's quite satisfied, however, that none of the injuries was inflicted after the fall. In any case, he considers that the shock alone would have been enough to kill her.'

'Somebody give her a shove?'

'Oh, no, sir! It was a much more carefully set up job than that. I don't think there's any doubt but that this was a matter of cold-blooded, deliberate murder. Somebody had fastened a length of fine wire across the top of the stairs, here outside your room. Anybody going either up or down would almost certainly have tripped over it and gone crashing down the stairs. It's a long, steep flight, sir, and . . .'

'You're telling me!' grumbled Dover.

'. . . and anyone plunging down like that would have been extremely lucky not to be killed. It looks as though Mrs Boyle was ascending the stairs when she tripped. She actually broke the wire but she still must have lost her footing in the dark – and that was that.'

'In the dark?' Dover stopped digging the marmalade out with his butter knife. 'I left the light on.'

'I fancy the murderer must have switched it off again, sir. With the only switch being here at the top of the stairs, Mrs

Boyle had no choice but to come up in the dark. I was the first on the scene, sir, after the screams, and the staircase was in darkness then. I'm afraid Mr Lickes is going to have to answer some very awkward questions at the inquest. I can see the coroner wanting to know why there wasn't another light switch at the bottom of the stairs. Mr Lickes's excuse that our two rooms are hardly ever used isn't going to be very acceptable, I'm afraid.'

'Yes,' grunted Dover. 'Well, let's not waste any time snivelling over Lickes's trouble. We've got enough of mine to sweat about. Now – this bit of wire. Suppose somebody had been at the top of the stairs, coming down and with the light on – would the wire have tripped him then?'

MacGregor looked thoughtfully at 'somebody' and nodded his head. 'Almost certainly, sir. It was very cunningly placed, though whether this was by accident or design, we don't know.'

'What do you mean – you don't know?' asked Dover, moodily pouring himself out another cup of tea.

'It's the hook that was screwed in the wall, sir. The murderer didn't bore a special hole for it. He merely inserted it in a crack in the woodwork that was already there. So the fact that he got his wire stretched across at just the right height and everything could be a lucky coincidence.'

'I like your idea of luck!' snarled Dover. 'You wouldn't be so bloody detached about everything if it was your neck in the firing line.' By a natural progression of ideas, Dover suddenly realized that he was sitting right in front of the window with only MacGregor's body between him and certain death. Any Charlie out there in the grounds with a high-velocity, telescopic-sighted rifle could . . . He got up and went and sat on the bed. 'Strewth, you needed eyes in the back of your head at this game!

MacGregor blushed for him. 'Would you like a cigarette, sir?' he asked, recalling that tobacco was supposed to be a sovereign remedy for the blue funk.

Dover, however, was not going to be caught napping as easily as that. 'You light it,' he ordered, 'and have a few drags first.'

'Oh, sir,' laughed MacGregor awkwardly, 'you don't really think . . .'

'I bloody well do! Look, after I came up to bed last night, some bastard came creeping out, fixed that wire up and put the light off. Well, he wasn't setting traps for flipping rabbits, was he? Here,' – he broke off this masterly analysis of the criminal mind to snatch the cigarette out of MacGregor's mouth – 'there's no need to puff it down to a blooming dog end! 'Strewth,' – he filled his lungs and erupted into a series of hacking coughs – 'you don't half smoke some cheap muck!'

MacGregor declined to be side-tracked into a discussion about the quality of the cigarettes he purchased for his superior officer's consumption. 'You were saying about the murderer, sir.'

'I don't need you to tell me what I was saying, laddie,' snapped Dover, spacing the words out between further coughs. 'The day I can't out-remember you, you can nail the lid down on me. That wire was put up for one of two people: you or me. Well, nobody's going to get out of a warm bed on a cold night just to snuff you out, are they?'

'Detective Inspector Stokes is working on the theory that Mrs Boyle was the intended victim, sir.'

'More fool him! Who'd want to croak old Ma Boyle?'

'She was a rather unpopular lady, sir.'

'And why should anybody expect her to be coming up those stairs? Nobody could have foreseen that. There's only your room and mine up here.'

MacGregor got his cigarette case out again and slowly lit himself a cigarette. He needed time to think. If he didn't choose his words very carefully, Dover would just go clean through the roof. Well, actually he would, anyhow, once he understood. 'The local police have a sort of tentative theory about that, too, sir.'

'Oh?'

MacGregor steeled himself. He managed a silly grin. 'It involves casting you as the murderer, sir. Of course,' he added diplomatically as Dover's pasty face took on a brilliant purple hue, 'they allow you were probably drunk at the time.'

Even Dover's ravings eventually ran out of steam. Two more cigarettes and a cup of cold tea helped to abate the fury but MacGregor had to wait until physical exhaustion set in before he could continue.

'I felt it was only fair to warn you what you were up against, sir. The whole thing is absolutely ridiculous, of course, but it's no good our burying our heads in the sand, is it?'

'I'd like to bury your head in boiling oil!' came the ungracious rejoinder. 'Of course, I might have expected it. Let you out of my sight for a couple of minutes and you're stabbing me in the bloody back. Anybody else'd have given this What's-his-name a punch up the bracket.'

'I hardly think that would have helped much, sir. You see, it's not just Inspector Stokes. It's all the witnesses.'

'Witnesses?' howled Dover. 'What bloody witnesses? My God, I'm being framed! How can there be any witnesses when I didn't so much as lay a fist on the old bitch?'

MacGregor pulled up a chair and sat down next to the bed. 'Listen, sir, the local police know all about your feud with Mrs Boyle. The way they see it, you upset her by making a noise late at night and she retaliated by publicly insulting you in the hotel dining-room. Last night, things went a stage further.' MacGregor stole a glance at Dover's face. 'It's no good looking like that, sir. Everybody in the hotel heard the pair of you banging about after we came in. The idea is that, round about half past one this morning, Mrs Boyle went on the offensive again. She'd sworn that she would stop at nothing to get the better of you.'

'She'd a hope!' bragged Dover half-heartedly. 'I could have flattened her with one hand tied behind my back!'

MacGregor nobly refrained from pointing out that this was

more or less what Dover was being accused of. 'For motives which we shall probably never be able to uncover now,' he went on, 'she made her way up to your room. Now, according to the theory that you are the murderer, you anticipated this nocturnal visit and put the wire across the stairs to kill her.'

'But why me?' whined Dover. 'I wasn't the only one who couldn't stomach the stinking old battle-axe. What about the Kettering woman?' he demanded, tossing conventional standards of loyalty to the winds. 'She's got one of those magic doll things of old Mother Boyle and she passes the time sticking pins in it.'

MacGregor looked purposefully out of the window. 'Yes, Miss Kettering has told them all about that, sir. She has also informed them that you visited her room last night and yourself stuck a pin in the model.'

'Female Judas!' growled Dover. ''Strewth, you can't trust anybody these days!'

'She also told them about the liqueur chocolates you ate, sir.'

'What the hell's that got to do with anything?'

'They think they may have made you a bit tiddly, sir. You ate nearly a pound and, on top of the wine you had at the Studio . . .'

Dover stuck his lower lip out and started thinking. If there was one activity at which he excelled, having had a fair amount of practice, it was saving his own skin. And, underneath that mountain of indolent flesh, there was even a tiny little detective who occasionally managed to struggle out. Dover swung round on MacGregor. 'What about the wire and the screw?'

'Well, it's early days yet, sir, for tracing where they came from. They're just ordinary things you can buy in any shop.'

'Buy?' – Dover pounced on the word. 'You mean they're new?'

'Oh yes, sir. Well, unused anyhow. Personally, from the look of them, I would say they were brand new.'

'And where am I supposed to have got them from?'

'Ah,' – MacGregor smiled with relief at being able to convey some more cheerful news – 'that's a strong point in your favour, sir. I've been able to vouch for the fact that you couldn't possibly have purchased them since you came to Sully Martin. And they're hardly the sort of thing you'd have brought with you, are they, sir? Actually, Superintendent Underbarrow' – he permitted himself a patronizing smirk – 'suggested that you might have pinched them from the murder bag. However, I was able to reassure him on that point.'

MacGregor need say no more. Both he and Dover knew perfectly well that the murder bag which MacGregor lugged round from investigation to investigation contained nothing more lethal than a few empty beer bottles, a broken pair of tweezers and the 1934 edition of *A Police Constable's Guide To His Daily Work*. This is not what murder bags are supposed to contain but at least MacGregor had managed to stop Dover using the one they had been issued with for his dirty washing.

'Well, that settles it,' said Dover comfortably. He considered that more than enough time had been spent on red herrings whose trail could only lead to him being stuck in the dock. 'Now all we've got to do is finger the collar of the blighter who was trying to nobble me. Bloody cheek! I'm warning you, I'll break his blooming neck when I get my hands on him. Well,' – he barked angrily at MacGregor – 'what are you dithering about at now? You can't still think Mrs Boyle was the intended victim.'

MacGregor shook his head. 'No, sir, I must admit it doesn't really seem likely. I can't believe that anybody could have known she was going to come up those stairs last night. On the other hand, though, anyone would be perfectly justified in working on the assumption that you would come down them.'

'I'm glad you're showing a bit of gumption at last,' said Dover. 'Pity your thinking's as sloppy as ever.'

'Sir?'

'The only ones who'd know for sure that I'd probably have to get up in the middle of the night are the bastards in this apology for an hotel. That narrows the field down for a start.' He began to tick off the names on his stubby fingers. 'There's Lickes and his wife, Pile and his daughter, that senile old idiot with his deaf aid, Miss Whatever-her-name-is that wouldn't say boo to a gander and ' – his lips drew back in a snarl – ' the Kettering woman. Now that's one I wouldn't mind having a bet each way on. Look how she enticed me into her room last night and forced all those chocolate things on me. Any fool could have guessed that they'd play merry hell with my stomach.' A look of bewilderment passed over his face. 'The funny thing is, though – they haven't! Oh, God,' – he slumped miserably back on to his pillows – ' I'll bet she's gone and constipated me, the silly cow!'

MacGregor's mind was still on his work. 'I'm afraid it's not quite as simple as that, sir.'

'You're telling me!' agreed Dover bitterly. 'Without a word of a lie, I've had every specialist in Harley Street scratching his head over my constipation before now. They just can't fathom out what . . .'

'No, sir. I meant that we can't restrict the murder suspects to the people in this hotel. I'm afraid your – er – difficulties are pretty widely known throughout the whole of Sully Martin.'

'They are?' Dover didn't quite know whether to be pleased or not. 'Who told you that?'

'Miss Wittgenstein, sir. Apparently Mrs Lickes is a bit of a gossip and she's been discussing the state of your – er – health when she's out shopping. Of course, in a little village like this, sir, you are rather a celebrity and it's only likely that people will take an interest in everything you do. Like a pop star, really, or royalty.'

'Oh?' Dover decided to be pleased 'Well, I suppose it's understandable.'

'What it boils down to, sir, is that practically anybody in Sully Martin could have stretched that wire across the stairs.

143

They'd have known from Mrs Lickes that your room was on the second floor and that you were likely to go downstairs at least once during the night.'

Dover frowned. He didn't care much for the sound of this. Apart from the fact that it smacked of a hell of a lot of work, it made him look so unpopular. 'Hold your horses, laddie,' he said. 'How would an outsider get into the hotel, eh? Any signs of a break-in?'

'No, sir.'

'Well, there you are then, aren't you?'

'Not quite, sir. You see there was no need to break in. The front door was left open.'

'What? All blooming night? It's a wonder we weren't all murdered in our beds!'

'I'm afraid I'm responsible, sir,' said MacGregor, deciding he might as well accept the blame before Dover shoved it on to him.

'You would be!'

'Mr Lickes left the door open for us last night, sir, and unfortunately I didn't think to lock it when we came in. As a matter of fact, what with fumbling round in the dark and everything, I didn't even close it. Anybody could have hung around out in the grounds, say, until all the bedroom lights went out and then just crept into the hotel and fixed the wire.'

'Marvellous!' said Dover. 'Bloody marvellous!' He would doubtless have gone on to mine this vein of constructive criticism further if he hadn't been put off his stroke by a knock at the door. 'What's that?' He clutched a pillow to his chest in a panic-stricken search for comfort and protection.

The door-handle was rattled impatiently.

''Strewth!' croaked Dover. 'They're trying to break in!'

Outside on the landing Superintendent Underbarrow knocked again. 'Anybody at home?' he shouted.

MacGregor got to his feet. 'It's Superintendent Underbarrow, sir. Shall I let him in?' He held out his hand for the key.

Dover fished around reluctantly in his pockets. Old Wheelbarrow was probably all right but there was no future in taking needless risks. ' Frisk him first! ' he ordered.

' Oh, *sir!* ' MacGregor accepted the key and, stoutly resolving that wild horses wouldn't make him search a senior police officer for concealed weapons, unlocked the door.

Superintendent Underbarrow breezed in. ' Well, now,' he asked jovially, ' and how's our Number One Suspect, eh?'

Dover snorted in disgust. ' Oh, very funny! '

' Just the lads downstairs having a bit of a joke,' chuckled the superintendent. ' A mite naughty of 'em, I'll admit, but your sergeant here was looking so solemn and po-faced they just couldn't resist pulling his leg.' He twinkled benevolently at MacGregor. ' You need a sense of humour in this job, sergeant.'

' So it seems sir,' said MacGregor stiffly. ' I must say that I got the impression that you were making a serious accusation.'

' Against a detective chief inspector from Scotland Yard?' asked Superintendent Underbarrow with a grin. ' That'll be the day, eh?'

' But the evidence of the other people in the hotel, sir. They said . . .'

' They said a lot of things, sergeant, none of which amounted to anything. I don't know what you fellows up in London do but, down here in the backwoods, we bumpkins don't start applying for murder warrants just because a bunch of old dodderers start getting spiteful. No,' – Superintendent Underbarrow settled himself on the foot of the bed – ' we've been talking it over downstairs and we've come to a pretty well unanimous conclusion. Of course, we're keeping an open mind as to the other possibilities but I don't think there's much doubt about it. Poor Mrs Boyle was murdered by mistake. They were really after your boss here.'

' I told you so! ' trumpeted Dover. He turned to Superintendent Underbarrow. ' Well, and what are you doing about it?'

' We're continuing our investigations, of course, and . . .'

'Continuing your investigations?' howled Dover. 'My bloody life's in danger and all you're doing is continuing your investigations?'

'We're keeping a constable on guard at the bottom of the stairs,' explained Superintendent Underbarrow easily. 'Don't worry, old chap, we'll look after you.'

'Suppose they try again?'

'Then we'll catch 'em,' said the superintendent with a quiet confidence that was clearly not infectious. 'Actually, that's more or less what I've popped up to see you about. It's really Inspector Stokes's job, of course, but he's a bit tied up at the moment so I said I'd give him a hand. You see, there's no two ways about it. The best protection we can give you is to collar this joker before he gets a second chance at you.'

'Well, you won't collar him lolling up here on your backside!' snarled Dover who could see himself lying in a pool of blood while this pack of gibbering idiots discussed the weather over his corpse.

'Of course not,' agreed Superintendent Underbarrow soothingly. He'd met people with cold feet before and reckoned he knew how to deal with them. 'But we'll need your help, won't we? If anybody's likely to know who's gunning for you, it's you yourself, isn't it? Now, you just have a bit of think about it. Who's got it in for you?'

'Ah,' said Dover, beginning to relax, 'now you're asking, aren't you?'

'I imagine you've made a good few enemies in your time,' prompted the superintendent dryly.

Dover preened himself. 'Hundreds. Thousands, probably. It's the penalty you have to pay for being successful. Why, half the crooks behind bars at this very moment are there because of me. And then there are all the ones who've done their time. Oh, the country must be swarming with villains who've got a grudge against me. You can't really blame them,' he added with phoney generosity. 'If it hadn't been for me outwitting 'em, they'd be walking around free as air.'

'Yes,' said Superintendent Underbarrow dubiously. 'So you think it could be a bit of your past catching up with you?'

'I wish I had a pound for every time I've been threatened with vengeance, by golly I do! I'd be a rich man now, I can tell you.'

MacGregor listened with wide-eyed incredulity. During his association with the chief inspector – which was admittedly nothing like as long as it felt – you could number his successful cases on the fingers of one hand. Crooks who could claim that they'd been outwitted by Dover must be very few and far between. Of course, he had brought a few cases to a satisfactory conclusion but that only proved that there were some baddies who were even more thick-headed than he was. Oh, yes – MacGregor repressed a wicked grin – and there was that poor devil of a murderer who was so exasperated by Dover's bumbling inefficiency that he'd actually confessed to put an end to it.

MacGregor surfaced from his scurrilous reminiscences to find that Superintendent Underbarrow was looking at him. 'I'm sorry, sir. Did you say something?'

'I was just wondering if you could help us out with a few names, sergeant.'

'Names, sir? Oh,' – MacGregor squirmed in some embarrassment – 'well, not offhand, sir.'

'Most of 'em were before his time!' snapped Dover before the superintendent could give expression to his evident surprise.

'Yes, come to think of it, I suppose they would be.' Superintendent Underbarrow scratched his chin thoughtfully. 'Well, we'll look into that aspect of it, of course, but I'd be surprised if we found any of your old sparring partners in Sully Martin. There aren't many strangers knocking around and none of the local people have ever been mixed in serious crimes, as far as I know. I suppose' – he looked questioningly at Dover – 'you'd recognize the fellow if you'd ever seen him before?'

'Never forget a face,' bragged Dover.

147

Superintendent Underbarrow leaned back against the foot of the bed. 'I must say I'd have thought we'd have done a bit better to start looking nearer home.'

Dover's heart missed a beat. Nearer home? God, why hadn't he thought of that before? He went cold as he thought of the risks he'd been running. Talk about nursing a viper in your bosom! Of all the ungrateful young bastards!

Superintendent Underbarrow was rather disconcerted to find that Dover was sliding down the bed towards him, pulling some very peculiar faces as he did so.

'Get rid of him!' mouthed Dover.

'What?'

Dover flapped his hands wildly and then tried to enjoin silence by placing one fat finger warningly across his lips.

MacGregor, intrigued by the soft scuttlings going on behind him, turned round.

Dover greeted him with a cheery smile. 'Ah, sergeant,' he said quickly, trying to look unconcerned, 'there's – er – something I want you to do for me.'

'What's that, sir?'

The cheery smile ripened as Dover endeavoured to think of something. 'Mrs Boyle's handbag!' he gasped desperately as he blurted out the first thing that came into his head.

'Mrs Boyle's handbag, sir?'

'That's right, sergeant.'

MacGregor had schooled himself over the years to be surprised at nothing. If the old fool wanted Mrs Boyle's handbag, presumably he could have it. 'Very good, sir. Do you want me to get it now?'

'Please!' cooed Dover, so distraught that he didn't even choke over the word.

MacGregor left the bedroom and, as soon as the door was shut behind him, Dover flung himself on Superintendent Underbarrow.

'Quick!' he hissed. 'Before he comes back!'

The superintendent was an exceptionally well-adjusted man

and he resolutely rejected the obvious explanation for this passionate assault. Very calmly and quietly he tried to loosen Dover's grip on his arm. 'Now, steady on, old chap! There's nothing to get worked up about.'

'Nothing to get worked up about?' screamed Dover. 'You great gibbering oaf! You let me get shut up in here all alone with a murderer and all you can think of is to tell me not to get worked up!'

Superintendent Underbarrow continued to play it cool. 'Now, suppose you just calm down and tell me all about it, eh?'

Dover took the advice and a deep breath. You had to remember that these plough-boys weren't as bright in the head as the rest of us. He caught Superintendent Underbarrow by the lapels and gave him a good shake. 'MacGregor! You've got to do something about MacGregor! It's your duty!'

'Well, now, and what would you like me to do, eh?'

''Strewth!' groaned Dover. He gritted his teeth. 'I want you to arrest him, you silver-buttoned dummy! Damn it all, you've just said he was trying to kill me.'

'I did?'

'All right, all right,' said Dover in the hope that a bit of soft soaping might do the trick, 'it was very clever of you. It never crossed my mind, I'll admit that. I knew he was a treacherous little brute but . . . The young bastard, I'll bet he's been planning this for years.'

Superintendent Underbarrow took his time and thought it all over very carefully. Then he got it. 'You old devil!' he chuckled, digging Dover appreciatively in the ribs. 'Tit for tat, eh? Paying me back in my own coin? Well, I suppose I asked for it. You'd certainly got me fooled there for a minute. Fancy trying to con me that your sergeant's the murderer!'

'Me? You bloody fool, you're the one who said that.'

'When?'

'Just now, for God's sake. You sat there as large as life and twice as ugly and said I ought to look nearer home.'

'Yes, but I didn't mean Sergeant MacGregor,' protested Superintendent Underbarrow, beginning to feel distinctly uncomfortable. 'Good heavens, it never even occurred to me.'

'Well, who did you mean?'

Superintendent Underbarrow got his handkerchief out and passed it slowly across his brow. 'The chap who murdered Walter Chantry, of course,' he explained. 'It looks as plain as the nose on your face to me. A place as small as Sully Martin's hardly likely to have two murderers running around loose at the same time, is it?'

Ten

MacGregor came trailing back up the stairs with Mrs Boyle's handbag. He'd had quite a job getting hold of it as all the murdered woman's belongings had already been inventoried by the efficient local police and placed under lock and key. Inspector Stokes, to whom the request had eventually been referred, had made a lot of difficulties. He'd only just finished putting the seals on the door of Mrs Boyle's bedroom and had no intention of breaking them open again if he could possibly help it.

'What on earth does he want it for?' he asked, reluctantly fingering his penknife.

MacGregor retreated behind a mysterious smile and shook his head.

'Aw, come off it!' pleaded Inspector Stokes. 'We're all on the same side, aren't we? You see,' – he gazed at the strips of tape and the sealing wax which he had affixed with such loving care – 'I'll have to put something in the report about why I opened the door again. It'd help if I had a proper sort of reason.'

'How about "Detective Chief Inspector Dover wished to examine Mrs Boyle's handbag"?' suggested MacGregor unhelpfully.

'There's a good shilling's worth of sealing wax on there,' Inspector Stokes grumbled. 'To say nothing of the tape. Money down the drain and my chief constable in the middle of an economy drive. You see how I'm fixed, don't you? You'll be back safe and sound in London while I'm on the carpet trying to account to the old man for two and ninepence worth of assorted items of expendable stationery.'

'Sorry,' said MacGregor.

Inspector Stokes opened his penknife and inserted the blade tentatively under one of the seals. He paused. 'Here, your boss isn't on to something, is he?'

'He's waiting for that handbag sir.'

Inspector Stokes removed the blade from under the seal. 'I don't get this,' he said. 'I thought we were all agreed that Mrs Boyle was killed by mistake. Well, if she was, what's so important about her handbag?'

'I'm afraid I can't say sir.'

'Can't or won't?' Inspector Stokes jabbed crossly at the seals and prised them off. 'Well, I'll have something to say about this in my report and I shan't mince my words. Two can play at being uncooperative and you can tell your chief inspector that with my compliments.'

'If I don't get that handbag soon, sir,' said MacGregor, 'he'll be down here and you can tell him yourself.'

Inspector Stokes turned the key in the lock. 'I shall subject that handbag to a thorough examination,' he announced with dignity, 'before I surrender it.'

And he did. MacGregor, who was consumed by an equal curiosity, helped him. Neither of them were one whit the wiser when they'd finished.

'It'd be a help,' observed Inspector Stokes tartly as he shovelled the contents back in, 'if we knew what we were looking for.' He shook his head in bewilderment. 'Why do you think she was carting five pairs of scissors round with her?'

'Sentimental value, sir?' suggested MacGregor, getting his

hands on the bag at last and snapping it shut. 'Well, thank you very much.'

'Just a minute!' said Inspector Stokes. 'I want a signature first.'

As soon as he got back to Dover's bedroom, MacGregor sensed that things were a bit fraught. The two senior police officers were sitting in grim silence and studiously avoiding looking at each other. MacGregor gave Dover the handbag.

'Well,' said Superintendent Underbarrow with a painfully unnatural casualness, 'I think I'd better be running along.' He stood up and addressed a painting of Lake Windermere in autumn which was hanging on the wall. 'You'll let me know if there's anything you want doing?'

Dover emptied the contents of Mrs Boyle's handbag out on the bed and began poking through them. Now – what was it that Kettering woman had said?

MacGregor waited a fraction too long to see if Dover was going to answer the question. 'Yes, of course, sir,' he gabbled hurriedly as Superintendent Underbarrow's blood pressure rose. 'Thank you very much indeed, sir. We're most grateful for your co-operation.'

'I'll see you get copies of all our reports,' said Superintendent Underbarrow stiffly, 'and our chaps'll finish off the routine investigations they're doing.'

Dover's fat hands closed greedily on a bottle which, according to its home-made label, contained cough mixture. His face broke into a gratified smile as the memory of Miss Kettering's words came flooding back to him.

'That's very kind of you, sir.' Out of the corner of his eye MacGregor watched the superintendent surreptitiously watching Dover.

'We'll have to clear it with the chief constable first,' said Superintendent Underbarrow absently as Dover removed the cork from the cough mixture with his teeth, 'but I think you

can take it as definite that the investigation is now your responsibility.'

MacGregor murmured his appreciation without really taking
in what was being said. He was far more interested in Dover,
who now tipped the bottle up and poured a generous quantity
of the contents down his throat.

'Oooowagh!' gasped Dover, wiping his lips appreciatively
on the back of his hand. 'That hit the spot, all rightie!'

The aroma of fine old Scotch whisky wafted gently through
the room.

Superintendent Underbarrow took his leave.

'And good riddance to bad rubbish!' sniggered Dover as
the superintendent's footsteps faded away down the stairs.
'He should stick to waggling his arms at motor cars, that one,
and leave the detective work to them that's got the brain for
it.'

'What exactly did he mean, sir, when he said that the investigation's now our responsibility?'

'What do you think he meant, moron?' asked Dover, apparently quite unmellowed by Mrs Boyle's medicinal whisky.
'They reckon the two cases are linked, don't they? Whoever
tried to murder me was the same one that did for Chantry.'
He took another swig out of his bottle and smacked his lips
with gusto.

'I see, sir.'

Dover's eyes wandered idly over the contents of Mrs Boyle's
handbag and came to rest with an almost audible click on a
nicely bulging wallet.

MacGregor put a stop to that before the temptation proved
irresistible. 'Excuse me, sir, but all the money and everything's been very carefully counted.'

Dover withdrew his hand and tried to look as though the
idea had never entered his head. That was the trouble with
police work these days, he thought indignantly – too much
checking and counter-checking.

'And you agree with Superintendent Underbarrow, sir?'

'What about?'

MacGregor prayed for patience. 'About the two cases being connected, sir.'

'Of course,' said Dover, through a jaw-cracking yawn. 'It's the only logical explanation.' He finished off the rest of the whisky and gave vent to his appreciation with a loud belch. 'Besides, it'll keep that bunch of muck-spreading clod-hoppers out of our hair.'. He stuck the cork back in the empty bottle and tossed it down on the bed.

'You intend to handle the investigation yourself, sir?'

Dover's eyelids began to droop. 'What else?' he replied sleepily. 'I'm the one who was damned near murdered, aren't I?'

'But sir . . .'

Dover began to get fractious. 'I do wish you'd stop yacking for five minutes,' he whined. 'Why don't you make yourself useful and push off for a bit? I've had a very disturbed night, you know.'

MacGregor wasn't exactly a worm but even he had his turning point. If he didn't do something drastic he could see himself mouldering on in Sully Martin until he was eligible for his pension. The idea of Dover, who was as near to solving the murder of Walter Chantry as he was to flying to the moon, blithely taking on a second case was almost more than flesh and blood could endure. No, subservience and deference were all very well in their way but the time had come when Dover must be saved from himself. Surely even he would be grateful to be spared the humiliation of not catching his own murderer?

There was a cold glint in MacGregor's eye as he glanced at the recumbent lump on the bed. Sometimes you had to be cruel to save your sanity. He turned resolutely on his heel and marched out of the bedroom.

Ten minutes later he was back again, with a large mug of strong black coffee. He put the mug down on the dressing-table while he flung the bedroom window open to its widest extent and then soaked the bit of old rag Dover apparently used as a facecloth in cold water. This done, he stormed over to the bed, shook Dover until his dentures rattled, dragged him into a sitting position and slapped the ice-cold cloth over his face.

'Oh, heck!' moaned Dover, flapping feebly as MacGregor retreated out of range. 'What's going on?'

MacGregor was back at the bed-side again. He whipped the damp cloth off Dover's face and plastered it across the top of his head. 'Drink this!' he shouted.

Dover goggled at the steaming cup which was thrust under his nose. 'Warisit?' he enquired.

'Never mind what it is! Drink it!'

Thoroughly cowed, Dover did as he was told. 'It's horrible!' he complained.

MacGregor turned a deaf ear. He was too busy arranging a hard upright chair squarely in the path of the young gale that was blowing through the open window. When this was settled to his satisfaction, he swept across to the bed again. 'Finished?'

Dover gulped down the last mouthful and the mug was snatched from his hands. 'Here,' he began as MacGregor got him by the scruff of the neck and dragged him off the bed, 'what the blue blazes do you think you're . . .'

'You'll be much more comfortable over here, sir,' panted MacGregor, manhandling his chief inspector over to the window and dropping him unceremoniously on the waiting chair. 'You and I are going to have a little conference.'

'A conference?'

'That's right!' MacGregor pulled up another chair and sat down facing Dover. 'It's what detectives have from time to time, particularly when their investigations grind to a complete halt.'

'Hey, watch it, laddie!' growled Dover, rallying a bit as the fresh air and black coffee started getting through to him. 'I've no objection to you showing a bit of initiative for once in your life but don't start coming the old sarcastic with me.'

'I beg your pardon, sir,' apologized MacGregor, 'but I do feel we've got to do something. We've got two murders on our hands now – Walter Chantry and Mrs Boyle – and we just aren't getting anywhere with either of them. I'm merely suggesting that we try and work out some plan of action.'

Dover turned his coat collar up. 'Well, we're not going to bust a gut avenging Walter Chantry, for a start. It's the joker who tried to get me that matters. I'll make him rue the day he was born, don't you worry!'

MacGregor sighed. It was like trying to quarry through solid granite with a toothpick. 'I thought we'd already agreed, sir, that the same person was responsible for both crimes.'

'Eh? Oh, well, that's what I said, wasn't it? Of course it's the same fellow. It's a question of motive, isn't it? He was trying to rub me out before I nabbed him for the murder of Chantry.'

MacGregor got that old sinking feeling as they approached the frontier of Cloud Cuckoo Land. 'I don't think that can be quite right, can it, sir?'

'Why not?'

'Well, you're not going to nab him for the murder of Walter Chantry, are you?'

'But I must be!' protested Dover. 'Why else is he gunning for me? He's panic-stricken, you see. He's running scared. He knows that any minute now I'm going to . . .'

'But you're not!' insisted MacGregor, hoping that if he said it three times Dover would realize it was true. 'Look, sir, let's be perfectly frank about this. Neither you nor I has the least idea who murdered Chantry, have we?'

Dover's bottom lip stuck out truculently. 'I've got my theories,' he muttered. His face cleared. 'In fact, I reckon I've probably got the answer, really, but I just haven't fitted the pieces together yet.'

MacGregor let his shoulders slump as his worst fears were fully confirmed. Dover, as usual, just hadn't got a clue. 'It's going to be a race, isn't it, sir?'

' A race?'

'Between you and the murderer, sir. Whether you unmask him before he kills you.' MacGregor didn't appear to find the prospect entirely distasteful.

' Oh, charming!' said Dover. He shivered. ' Here, let's have that bloody window shut. I don't want to go catching pneumonia on top of everything else.'

MacGregor got up and closed the window with the air of one granting the condemned man's last request. ' Of course, we'll give you all the protection we can, sir – for what it's worth. Unfortunately a clever, ruthless, desperate man isn't easy to stop. He's nothing to lose and everything to win.'

''Strewth!' groaned Dover. 'You're a right Job's comforter, you are.'

Delicately MacGregor began to bait the hook. ' The solution's in your own hands sir.'

' You're damned right it is!' snorted Dover, wresting the bait, hook, line, sinker and rod clean out of his sergeant's grasp. ' I'm catching the first bloody train back to London! Where did you put my suitcase?'

' But you can't turn tail and run, sir!'

' Want a bet?' Dover was on his feet and heading for the wardrobe. ' I'd sooner be a live donkey than a dead sitting-duck any old day of the week.' He dragged his overcoat off the hanger. ' I haven't lasted this long by playing the bloody hero.'

' And the Assistant Commissioner, sir?'

Dover, reaching up for his bowler hat, wavered. ' Stuff him,' he said with more bluster than conviction. He threw his overcoat back in the wardrobe and slammed the door.

Paradoxically, the Assistant Commissioner (Crime) might well have been delighted to see Dover beat an ignominious and shameful retreat back to London. It would have provided even more fuel for the secret dossier he had been compiling for years on Scotland Yard's most unwanted man. Indeed, rank cowardice in the face of the enemy might prove to be just the sort of ammunition the Assistant Commissioner (Crime) was waiting for.

Nobody knew better than Dover that, with his blemished record and shaky stature, he couldn't afford to take too many risks. There was a limit to what even the Metropolitan Police would tolerate. He gave the wardrobe a vicious kick and stumped miserably back to his chair.

' All right,' he snarled, ' what's your suggestion?'

MacGregor permitted himself a faint smile of relief. If only Dover would accept advice more often, they wouldn't get into quite so many messes. 'Well, sir, I propose that we really knuckle down and put our backs into it and find out who murdered Walter Chantry. That way we'll kill two birds with one stone. We'll solve the case and put an end to any further attempts on your life.'

' Solve the case, eh?' Dover was momentarily intrigued by the dazzling novelty of the idea but reaction soon set in. ' That's going to be easier said than done,' he pointed out.

MacGregor dusted off his most persuasive manner. 'Not really, sir. After all, you've already put your finger on our main advantage. The killer wouldn't have tried to murder you if he hadn't been pretty certain that you were on to him. That means that somewhere you must have a clue to his identity. All we have to do is find it.'

' But when I said that just now,' objected Dover, ' all you could do was pooh-pooh the idea.'

' Well, I just meant, sir, that it wasn't going to be as easy as all that. We're not going to get it handed to us on a plate, are we? We've got a lot of work to do first.'

Dover winced at the word ' work '. ' What have you got in mind?' he asked with a sigh.

' Well,' – MacGregor hitched his chair forward eagerly – ' I think we've just got to review all the evidence you've collected since we came here. Maybe, if we go through everything all, over again, we'll spot the slip or the discrepancy or whatever it is.'

'Blimey!' said Dover.

But MacGregor was not going to be denied. He pulled his notebook out and turned with an air of importance to a clean page. 'We'll stick to a chronological order, I think, sir. Now, who was the first person you interviewed yesterday afternoon?'

'I don't know,' grumbled Dover unhelpfully. 'Pile, was it? Or Lickes?'

'I think it was Mr Lickes, sir.' MacGregor wrote the name down in large capitals. He looked up. 'Can I get your notes for you, sir?'

'What notes?'

'The notes you took at the interview, sir.' One look at Dover's face provided the answer but MacGregor couldn't stop himself asking the question.

'How could I take notes when I was lying sick in bed?' howled Dover. 'You want it with blood on, you do.'

'Perhaps you can recall what Mr Lickes said, sir.'

Dover tried to find a more comfortable sitting position on his chair. 'Of course I can! He said that he and his missus got up after the earthquake and went out into the village. They met Pile and his daughter. Mrs Lickes brought the girl back here and Lickes stayed on to help with the rescue work.'

MacGregor's pencil hovered forlornly over his notebook. 'Is that all, sir?'

'That's the gist of it,' said Dover.

'Did he see Mr Chantry?'

'Says he didn't.'

'Well, did you gather anything about Mr Lickes's attitude to Mr Chantry, sir?'

'No,' said Dover, just for the pleasure of seeing the look on MacGregor's face. 'Well, there was something about turning this place into a motel. Lickes wasn't wild about the idea.'

'They quarrelled?'

'Not according to Lickes.' Dover wriggled around in an effort to ease his aching buttocks. 'You'll not find a motive for murder there, laddie. Lickes owns this hotel. He can please himself what he does with it. Chantry was just chucking out potty suggestions.'

'He might have threatened to open up another hotel in opposition, sir?' suggested MacGregor hopefully.

'And pigs might fly! Look, laddie, we're supposed to be solving a murder case, not making up fairy stories.'

MacGregor accepted the rebuke. 'Who did you see next, sir?'

'Pile,' said Dover, beginning to look bored. 'Now, he actually admits having seen Chantry so you can stick his name down.'

'But he was a friend of Chantry's, wasn't he, sir?' objected MacGregor. 'And would he kill a man who'd just rescued him and his daughter?'

'Stranger things have happened at sea.'

'Did he say anything else, sir?'

'Who?'

'Wing Commander Pile, sir.'

'Oh,' – Dover scratched his head in a burst of irritation – 'he complained about the goings on of that bunch of artists. All highly exaggerated,' he remembered crossly. 'Then,' he went on, determined to get all this over with as soon as possible, 'I saw Mrs Lickes. She'd nothing much to say, either.'

'But she confirmed her husband's story, sir?'

'They always do,' said Dover gloomily.

'Did she like Mr Chantry?'

Dover was beginning to stare blankly out of the window. There was a lengthy pause. 'Search me,' he said at last.

MacGregor recognized the danger signs. Even with his life in jeopardy, Dover was incapable of concentrating on anything for more than a couple of minutes at a time. MacGregor tried to revive the chief inspector's flagging interest. 'Should we try a different tack, sir?'

Dover blew wearily down his nose. 'I wish you'd make up your flipping mind.'

'I'm only trying to jog your memory, sir. If we keep talking about the case, something might just go click.'

'Something has!' Dover stood up and rubbed himself vigorously. 'My blooming spine! I've gone all numb sitting on that dratted chair.' His eyes began to swivel round to the bed.

'I thought if we worked out some kind of a timetable, sir,' said MacGregor hurriedly, 'and mapped out people's movements round about the vital time, we might . . .'

'A good idea!' approved Dover, stretching himself elaborately. 'Ooh, my poor old back! Yes, right – well, you carry on with that and I'll have a look at it when you've finished.' He took a casual step or two away from the window.

'I really think it would be better if we worked on it together, sir.'

'Of course, of course!' Dover reached the bed and sat down with the contentment of a homing pigeon. He plumped up the pillows. 'Anything you say, laddie.'

'We really must get on with it, sir!' protested MacGregor as Dover swung his feet up with an ecstatic grunt. 'Another attempt may be made on your life at any moment!'

Dover raised his head a couple of inches from the pillow. 'Just pull that eiderdown up over my feet, will you? There's one hell of a draught coming from somewhere. Ah,' – he sank back again – 'that's better. Now, you go right ahead and I'll chip in when you get stuck, eh?'

MacGregor ground his teeth with suppressed fury and, seizing his chair, crashed it down a couple of inches from Dover's nose. He settled himself on it and filled his lungs. 'The earthquake occurred at exactly two o'clock, sir,' he announced in ringing tones, 'and everybody with the exception of the three artists appears to have been in bed. We've got to allow people a few minutes to take in what was happening and then they begin to move. A lot of people, of course, like the regular guests in this hotel, didn't do anything which is of much interest to us. They didn't leave their homes, or if they did, they didn't go anywhere near the scene of the crime. In fact, because of the peculiar way the earthquake split the village in two, most of the inhabitants couldn't reach the scene of the crime at all until long after Chantry was dead, even if they'd wanted to.'

'Oh, quite,' murmured Dover, just to show that he was all ears.

'So that allows us to eliminate a large part of Sully Martin's population from the list of suspects. We can also eliminate a lot of other people, too, the victims who were killed or badly injured in the earthquake, the people who were looking after them until the rescue services arrived, those who are too young or too old to have committed the crime, and so on. I've checked and re-checked, sir, and, as I see it, we're really only left with seven: Mr and Mrs Lickes, Wing Commander Pile, Mr Oliver, Mr Lloyd Thomas, Miss Wittgenstein and young Mr Hooper.'

'Errors and omissions excepted,' agreed Dover, speaking as though he was very far away. He roused himself. 'Hasn't Mrs Lickes got an alibi?'

'Not much of one, sir. She could have returned to the disaster area much sooner than she says she did.'

'Was Chantry strangled from in front or behind?'

'From behind, sir. Does it matter?'

'I shouldn't think so. How tall was he?'

'About five foot ten, sir.'

Dover pursed his lips. 'Can't you scrub all the women?'

'He could have been kneeling down when he was attacked, sir. And Mrs Lickes is quite wiry. Miss Wittgenstein is pretty powerfully built, too, especially about the arms and shoulders.'

'It's kneading all that clay,' muttered Dover as he snuggled down again.

MacGregor pressed doggedly on. 'So, at two o'clock we have the earthquake and the first incident we know about after that is the collapse of Wing Commander Pile's house, trapping him and his daughter. Shortly after this, Walter Chantry makes his appearance on the scene when he rescues the Piles.

After that, he joins his son-in-law for a few minutes in the Sally Gate area and sends him away to get reinforcements. Nobody admits to seeing him alive again. Colin Hooper could have killed him then. Wing Commander Pile returned alone to his house to collect some clothes so he had a few minutes in which he could have found Chantry and murdered him. Mr Lickes is in pretty much the same boat. After he got separated from Colin Hooper, he'd got ample opportunity and he was in the right area of the village. Then we've got these three artists. They all knew roughly where Chantry was and none of them has much in the way of an alibi.' MacGregor bent forward so that his voice could blast straight down Dover's ear. ' Do you agree with me so far, sir?'

' I couldn't have put it better myself,' said Dover.

' And, now, we come to the question of motive.'

Dover hoisted himself up into a sitting position. ' Look,' he said, ' this is all very fine but I don't reckon it's getting us anywhere, do you? I'm the one that's supposed to have the key to the whole business but, with you rabbiting on like a babbling brook, I can't hear myself think. Now,' – he nudged the hint forward with an air of sweet reasonableness – ' why don't you push off for a bit and let me give my subconscious a chance?'

' Your subconscious, sir?'

' That's right!' said Dover, trying not to spoil it all by getting peevish. ' That's what you do when you can't remember something, isn't it? You just put it right out of your mind and let your subconscious spew it up. Now, if I was to lie here quietly and let my mind go a complete blank, I reckon that by the time you brought my lunch up I'd have the answer.'

MacGregor spared a brief moment to wonder whether Dover in a wheedling mood wasn't even more sickening than when he was shouting and bawling his head off. Not that it really mattered because, whichever way he played it, this was one time when he was not going to get his own way. ' I honestly don't think it's a very good idea, sir.'

' Well, luckily,' sneered Dover, reverting with all the ease in the world to a tougher line, 'it doesn't matter a row of two pins what you think. Shove off!'

MacGregor stood up. 'Very well, sir, but I think I ought to warn you that I am not going to bring your lunch up. And neither is anybody else. If you want something to eat, you're going to have to go down to the dining-room and have your meal there.'

'Have you gone clean out of your feeble little mind?' spluttered Dover. 'I'm giving you an order! You start coming your tricks with me, laddie, and I'll fix it so's your own mother won't recognize you!'

'I doubt if the board of enquiry would consider my carrying your lunch up a legitimate part of my duties, sir,' replied MacGregor smoothly.

Dover goggled. 'What board of enquiry?'

'The one that will be convened, sir, when I submit a formal complaint about your handling of this investigation. Amongst other things, I shall be charging you with professional incompetence, you see.'

'You'll not have much of a future in the force after that!' snapped Dover.

'You'll have none at all, sir.'

This simple statement of fact pulled Dover up sharp. 'You're bluffing,' he said sullenly.

'I shouldn't count on it, sir.'

'Then it's blackmail!'

'That's much more like it, sir,' agreed MacGregor calmly. 'Only for your own good, of course.'

'Oh, of course!' echoed Dover sarcastically. He scowled thoughtfully at his sergeant. That was the trouble with these starry-eyed, conscientious types – they'd no bloody sense of proportion. Fancy getting all worked up into a muck sweat over solving a lousy murder case! Still, there was no point in making a big issue out of it. Dover prepared to capitulate gracefully. 'You bloody kids think you know everything these days,' he growled.

MacGregor could recognize a white flag when he saw one. 'Part of my duty is to protect you, sir. When your life's in danger I can't in all conscience stand idly by and let you take unnecessary risks.'

Dover rather liked this line. 'Perhaps I am a bit careless about my personal safety,' he admitted ruefully. 'It's always been one of my failings. Well, laddie, what was it exactly you had in mind?'

MacGregor sat down again and looked at his watch. 'We've got nearly an hour before lunch, sir, so I suggest we use that time for discussing the motives of the various suspects. Then I propose that we go downstairs and have lunch. This will give you the opportunity to mix with some of the people we've got our eye on and – who knows? – you may just remember something. After lunch, I think we ought to go out and have a look at the scene of the crime. I don't think you've actually got round to doing that yet, have you, sir? Then we might call at the Studio again and perhaps have a word or two with the Hoopers.'

'It sounds fine,' said Dover bleakly.

MacGregor gave him a cigarette to sugar the pill. 'And now,' he went on, 'we come to the question of motive.' He opened his notebook again. 'Here, sir, I think we really must put Chantry's daughter and her husband at the top of the list. They've obviously got much the . . .'

Eleven

By the time he was let out for lunch – and with no remission
for good conduct – Dover had worked up a pretty good grudge
against MacGregor. This time young Charles Edward had
really gone too far. Dover wasn't quite sure exactly how he was
going to wreak his vengeance but he was confident that undiluted spite would find a way. Dover had never been subjected
to such torture in his entire career. Shut up all bloody morning talking shop! Well, not so much talking, when you came
to think about it, as listening. It was MacGregor who'd done
all the spouting, going on and on and on about the sudden
death of Walter Chantry – as if anybody cared. Dover had
several times tried to re-introduce the more beguiling topic
of his own near assassination but MacGregor had refused to
be diverted. The attack on Dover, he maintained, had been of
secondary and incidental importance. Dover's *amour propre*
was still smarting over that one. That he should have been reduced to playing second fiddle to the Walter Chantrys of this
world!

When he was finally released, Dover made MacGregor lead
the way downstairs, just in case. Even so he'd shied visibly
when he'd had to pick his way over the chalked outline of Mrs

Boyle's body. There, but for a touch of providential constipation...

The uniformed policeman on the landing saluted with reassuring deference and Dover descended into the entrance hall feeling a little better. There were signs of police activity everywhere. Another stalwart in blue was on duty by the front door and wires for the temporary telephones were festooned untidily across the ceiling. The door leading into the lounge was firmly closed and bore a large notice forbidding entry to unauthorized persons. Things seemed very quiet inside but, if you listened carefully, you could hear the gentle click of the dominoes and the soft shuffling of the playing cards. Outside in the drive a whole convoy of police cars held themselves in readiness while their drivers chatted and smoked in the watery sunshine.

'What,' sniffed Dover disparagingly, 'no dogs?'

MacGregor realized this was a joke. 'Don't let them hear you, sir, or they'll bring a whole pack up.'

'It looks about the only thing they haven't got,' grumbled Dover who naturally considered the scientific approach to detection more trouble than it was worth. 'We're not going to have all that mob guzzling with us in the dining-room, are we?'

'No, sir. I believe they've set up a mobile canteen round the back.'

'Thank God for that!'

Dover followed MacGregor towards the dining-room. Just as they drew near, the door opened and Wing Commander Pile came out. He brushed past them without a word and picked up the telephone receiver which was lying on the counter of the reception desk.

'Hello? Pile here.' He turned to watch Dover and MacGregor as they went into the dining-room. 'Well, no – since you ask – it is not a particularly convenient time. I was just about to have luncheon.'

Inside the dining-room everything looked remarkably normal – except for Mrs Boyle's empty chair and her fellow guests were all managing to reconcile themselves quite cheerfully to that. Miss Kettering and Miss Dewar had both draped themselves in black but they were chattering away together like a couple of excited schoolgirls.

'It's so much nicer than mine,' twittered Miss Kettering, 'and Mr Lickes says I can move in right after the funeral. Ah,' – she broke off to smile a welcome to Dover and Mac-Gregor – 'a very good morning to you! Isn't it nice to have the sun shining for a change?'

The tragic events of the night weren't getting old Mr Revel down either, though he, of course, could be relied upon to accept any casualties suffered by the monstrous regiment with great fortitude. He nodded his greeting to the two detectives. 'One down and two to go!' he shouted excitedly to the great indignation of Miss Kettering and Miss Dewar.

Mr Lickes skipped across and flicked a few crumbs off the tablecloth. 'Lunch will be a few minutes late,' he apologized. 'We've had rather a hectic morning, what with one thing and another.' He leapt for the sideboard, grabbed a tarnished silver dish and bounced back again. 'Have a bread roll while you're waiting!'

Dover and MacGregor obediently helped themselves and Mr Lickes was away again. He did a sort of comic goosestep over to the Piles' table and offered his dish to the girl, who was sitting there by herself. 'And how about you, young lady? We mustn't leave you out!'

The girl stared uncomprehendingly.

'Go on, Linda!' urged Mr Lickes. 'Have one!'

She glanced at the dining-room door and then, uncertainly, shook her head.

'Nonsense!' insisted Mr Lickes kindly. 'Your daddie won't mind. We can't have our most important guest suffering the pangs of hunger, now can we? That would never do!' He picked out a roll and put it in her hand. 'Tell you what,' he grinned, 'I'll try and find you a bit of butter in a minute. You'd like that, wouldn't you?'

The girl stuffed the roll in her mouth and gave a little nod.

'I thought so!' laughed Mr Lickes while Miss Kettering and Miss Dewar looked on with indulgent approval.

'Funny man!' said the girl.

Mr Lickes was delighted. 'Oh, so you think I'm funny, do you? Well, how about this, then?' He put his dish down, had a quick look round to see that he'd got enough room and turned a somersault.

Linda Pile clapped her hands and spurred Mr Lickes on to more acrobatic feats. He did a couple of cartwheels which sent the poor child into ecstasies.

'Isn't she sweet?' murmured Miss Kettering.

'Such a shame!' agreed Miss Dewar and dabbed her eyes.

Mr Lickes let rip with an allez-oop and stood on his head, peering up at Linda and pulling funny faces. Then he hoisted himself a little higher and began to walk, rather unsteadily, on his hands.

The performance began to get rather noisy and Mrs Lickes came out of the kitchen to see what on earth was going on. At the same time Wing Commander Pile came through the door from the entrance hall.

Wing Commander Pile must have had the gift of instant comprehension because he took the entire scene and its implications in at one glance: his daughter jumping about in unfeigned joy, Mr Lickes willingly making a fool of himself and everybody else watching.

'Stop that!' he roared.

Linda's giggles continued but the rest of the room fossilized into a shocked silence as Mr Lickes picked himself up off the floor.

Wing Commander Pile marched across and stood towering over his daughter. 'Be quiet, Linda!' he shouted.

The girl didn't seem to understand. She pointed at Mr Lickes. 'Funny man, Daddie!'

'I told you to shut up!' The wing commander had his hand half raised in a gesture that might have meant anything before MacGregor was out of his seat. Mr Lickes was nearer and quicker. He caught hold of the wing commander's arm.

Wing Commander Pile's face went black with fury. He whipped round and knocked Mr Lickes's hand away. 'Don't you touch me!' he snarled with such ferocity that Mr Lickes took a precautionary step backwards. 'And don't you dare speak to my daughter again, you . . . you performing monkey! I shan't warn you a second time!'

'Here, steady on!' stammered Mr Lickes.

Wing Commander Pile advanced on him, clenching his hands into useful looking fists. 'I'm sick to death of you hanging round her, you lecher! What's the matter – aren't there enough normal girls for you to paw about?'

'Here, I say!' protested Mr Lickes.

The wing commander turned back to his daughter. 'Come on, Linda!'

Linda's pretty face fell. 'Din-dins,' she said. A dribble of saliva began trickling down her face.

'We'll have luncheon in our rooms. Oh, do come along when you're told!' He reached across the table and dragged her to her feet. The laughter of a few minutes ago turned inevitably to tears, loud and uninhibited.

'Look,' said Mr Lickes, 'there's no need to . . .'

The wing commander continued to propel his squawling daughter out of the dining-room. 'There's every need!' he barked. He stopped for a moment to throw his next words straight into Mr Lickes's face. 'And don't you try creeping up on *me* in the dark! You might get rather more than you bargained for!'

'Never a dull moment,' said Dover as the door banged shut and MacGregor resumed his seat at their table.

'The man must be mad, sir.'

'Pile?' Dover tore a chunk off his bread roll and shoved it into his mouth. 'He's got a point, if you ask me. A child's mind in a woman's body? You can't blame him for taking a few precautions.'

A pale-faced Mr Lickes set the soup bowls down on the

table with a trembling hand. Dover watched with sly amusement. 'That's knocked a bit of the bounce out of him,' he observed.

MacGregor glanced at Mr Lickes as he served the other tables. 'You realize that Pile practically accused him of being the murderer, sir?'

Unfortunately Dover was already eating his soup and it is doubtful if MacGregor's softly worded question even penetrated the sound barrier. In any case, there was no response.

After lunch MacGregor still insisted that Dover should inspect the scene of the crime, in spite of having it very forcibly pointed out to him that the chief inspector's stomach was likely to react with unspeakable violence if it didn't get its postprandial nap.

'Nonsense, sir!' said MacGregor with all the callousness of the young and healthy. 'Fresh air and a bit of exercise will do you the world of good.'

Dover doubted this from the bottom of his heart but actually he was quite pleased to be getting out of the Blenheim Towers for a bit. Even he appreciated an occasional change of scenery.

MacGregor couldn't get the unpleasant scene in the dining-room out of his mind. 'I wonder if Lickes could be involved in Chantry's murder, sir?'

'Anything's possible,' grunted Dover, noting with disgust that they were back on that boring old subject again. 'If he is, his wife must be in cahoots with him.'

'Not necessarily sir. She'd come back to the hotel with the . . .'

Dover scowled. 'The attempt on me, you fool! You seem to be paying no blooming attention to that at all. Lickes couldn't have fixed that wire up in the middle of the night without his wife at least guessing what he'd been up to.'

'I suppose not, sir. I was wondering, though, if Lickes could be a bit of a lad for the ladies.'

'Oh, 'strewth!' groaned Dover.

'Perhaps it is a bit far-fetched, sir,' admitted MacGregor,

'but suppose Lickes was having an affair with somebody in the village and Walter Chantry found out about it. He threatens to expose Lickes and Lickes kills him.'

'You've got a mind like the wall of a public lavatory,' said Dover, stopping to give his feet a rest. 'Any proof that Lickes is a womanizer?'

'Well, only what Wing Commander Pile more or less hinted at just now, sir.'

Dover thought for a moment. 'How about Chantry being a sex maniac, the Don Juan of Sully Martin? He makes improper advances to the Pile girl and her father rises in wrath and clobbers him?'

'Oh, *sir!*' said MacGregor reproachfully.

'Look who's talking!'

They plodded on and eventually reached the bottom of the lane and turned into East Street. Outside the Studio was a small van and Miss Wittgenstein and Jim Oliver, watched by Lloyd Thomas, were loading a heavy box into it. Work stopped as the two detectives approached.

'Planning a moonlight flit?' asked Dover pleasantly as he rested his weight on the van's radiator.

'At two o'clock in the afternoon, goon?' Lloyd Thomas tucked his legs up so that Miss Wittgenstein could squeeze past him up the steps into the house. 'Why don't you do something socially acceptable for a change and give the lady a hand?'

Miss Wittgenstein appeared again, carrying another box. 'Oh, come on, you chaps! I don't want to miss that train.' She was surprised and gratified when MacGregor stepped forward to relieve her of her burden and put it in the back of the van. 'Oh, thanks very much!'

'Are you going away?' asked MacGregor as Jim Oliver sat down on the steps next to Lloyd Thomas.

'Oh, no – I'm just sending this batch of pots down to London. It's the first day we've managed to get any transport since the earthquake.' She patted one of the boxes proudly.

'Part of the export drive, you know. Would you like to see?'

MacGregor, being a nice young man, said he would and Miss Wittgenstein poked open one corner of the box, dug around in the straw and eventually brought out a newspaper-wrapped bundle. 'There you are!' she crowed as she stripped the covering off. 'Specially designed for the American market. Now, what do you think of that?'

'Very nice,' said MacGregor and gazed in some dismay at a rather nasty, mis-shapen beaker in thick pottery. He read the inscription, 'A Presente from ye olde Camelot'.

'Some of your best work,' said Jim Oliver loyally. He got up and came across, narrowing his eyes appreciatively. 'You've managed to get a really cosmic feeling into it.' He flourished a judicious thumb. 'That curve there – so chaste and yet so sur-feited.'

Lloyd Thomas shook his head pityingly.

'What's it for?' asked Dover, who was a complete Philistine where art was concerned and reckoned, in this instance, that a chimpanzee could have done better with its feet.

'It's not *for* anything,' explained Miss Wittgenstein patiently. 'It just is.'

Jim Oliver backed her up. 'A work of art doesn't need any justification, dear. You don't ask what the Mona Lisa is for, or the Sistine Chapel, do you?'

'No,' said Dover.

Miss Wittgenstein turned the mug round so that its wishy-washy brown and green glaze caught the sun. 'This is one for living with!' She looked at Dover. 'Would you like it?'

Dover wasn't one to turn down a free gift.

'Forty-nine and eleven,' said Miss Wittgenstein brightly.

MacGregor, after making what excuses, explanations and farewells he could, caught up with Dover as he reached the top of East Street. Things had been tidied up quite a bit since MacGregor's last visit, but the scene of ruin and devastation was still pretty breathtaking. Dover cut it down to size.

' I've seen worse,' he commented after standing and staring for a couple of minutes.

MacGregor was sorely tempted to ask where, but his attention was caught by a movement behind him. He turned just in time to see young Mrs Hooper beating as hasty a retreat as she was able to back through the front door of her house.

Dover had spotted her, too. 'Didn't want to meet us,' he grinned. 'I suppose in your book that's proof positive of a guilty conscience?'

'Not necessarily, sir,' said MacGregor, privately thinking that anybody who deliberately cultivated Dover's company wanted his or her head examining.

Dover grunted and resumed his contemplation of Sully Martin's big moment. MacGregor left him in peace for a few minutes. The last hour or so had not been totally useless. Dover had been given the chance to renew his acquaintance with nearly all of the chief actors in the drama. Only Colin Hooper had not put in an appearance and he was no doubt away at his work. MacGregor wasn't too distressed at his absence. He himself had been present at the encounter between Dover and the Hoopers and he was pretty certain that no vital snippets of evidence had slipped past him.

Dover looked round. He was actually looking for somewhere to sit down but MacGregor pounced eagerly on any flicker of interest or intelligence.

' Is anything stirring, sir?'

Dover glanced glumly down at his paunch. 'Not yet. I'll have to lay off liqueur chocolates if this is what they do to me.'

MacGregor restrained himself with difficulty. 'Well, actually sir, I really meant about the murder.'

' Oh, that,' said Dover.

' I was just wondering if, having seen everybody again, you might perhaps have recalled . . .'

' No,' said Dover.

There was a couple of minutes' silence out of respect for MacGregor's hopes.

'There's one thing,' said Dover, moving unhappily from one foot to the other. 'Why didn't you ask that bunch of layabouts what they were doing in the small hours of this morning?'

'The artists, sir? Oh, they've already been questioned by the local police.'

Dover snorted resentfully. 'You don't seem to be taking this attack on me very seriously.'

'I honestly think we'd do better to concentrate on the Chantry murder, sir.'

More minutes ticked by.

Dover sighed. 'How much longer are we going to stand here?' he demanded.

MacGregor gave himself a little shake. 'Wouldn't you like to see where Walter Chantry's body was found, sir?'

'No,' said Dover.

MacGregor gazed round in the hope of finding something that would keep Dover out of his bed for just a little longer. 'That's all that's left of Wing Commander Pile's house, sir.' He pointed to the heap of rubble directly in front of them. 'It must have been very nice before all this happened. The back half split clean away – you can see where the line of the fault ran – and collapsed almost immediately, I imagine. This front part, though, remained more or less standing. It was the demolition men who knocked it down. With the roof caved in and everything, it was just too risky to leave it standing. And ' – MacGregor turned round to indicate what he was talking about – 'there's Mr Chantry's house, only just across the road and practically undamaged. It's astonishing, really.'

'God moves in a mysterious way,' sneered Dover. 'His wonders to perform.'

MacGregor ignored the remark. 'Chantry and Colin Hooper would have come out of the front door, I imagine, sir, and Chantry would have come across the road about here somewhere to get to the Piles' house. Hooper must have gone off in that direction – towards the Sally Gate. Now, the three artists must have come out of the Studio over there and gone away from us, down East Street.' MacGregor frowned. ' I still think that's a bit funny, don't you, sir? I know it was dark and nobody knew what the dickens what going on but – to go right away from where all the damage was?'

Dover fidgeted uneasily. If he didn't look out, he'd be landed with yet another blow-by-blow account of the whole blooming business. He decided to break up MacGregor's rhythm. ' What's that?' he asked, pointing to a spot some-where to the left of where Wing Commander Pile's house had been.

MacGregor fell for it. ' Those houses, sir? Well, I think they were a row of farm labourers' cottages.' He began hunt-ing through his pockets for his large-scale plan of the village. ' I can tell you who lived there, sir, if I can just find . . . They were pretty badly damaged, as you can see, and several of the occupants were injured.'

Dover let MacGregor get his plan out and spread it out on the ground before saying calmly, ' Not the cottages.'

MacGregor, already down on his knees, looked up. ' Not the cottages, sir?'

Dover inclined his head towards a curved piece of kerbing stone which was still in place. ' Was there a road there, be-tween Pile's house and your precious cottages?'

' Er – yes, sir.' MacGregor flattened out his map again. ' It was a sort of continuation of East Street.' He peered at the plan. 'Yes, here we are – cutting North Street at right angles. Sidle Alley. Yes, I remember, sir. Superintendent Underbarrow mentioned it. It was just a sort of glorified cart track, really, running down by the side of Wing Commander Pile's house and curving left down the hill to where it joined the main road. I don't think it's of much interest to us, sir. There were no houses along it, only sheds and garages and things like that and, as you can see, it bore the brunt of the earthquake. The whole stretch must have virtually disappeared within seconds of the first tremor.'

' Sidle Alley?' muttered Dover, wrinkling his nose. 'Damn silly name.'

' Yes, sir,' said MacGregor.

A workman emerged from a temporary hut which had been erected a few yards away. He looked at Dover and MacGregor, decided they weren't snoopers from County Hall and went back inside again.

' We going to hang about here all day?' asked Dover.

' You've not thought of anything, sir?'

' No,' said Dover who held world ranking as a bare-faced liar.

MacGregor sighed and the pair of them began to wend their way back to the Blenheim Towers. The van was still standing outside the Studio but there was now no sign of any of the artists. Across the road, poor Millie Hooper mistimed it again. After waiting timidly in the kitchen for a good ten minutes, she had opted for the back door only to find that those horrid policemen were still there, spying on her. She fled back to the sanctuary of her kitchen and had hysterics.

MacGregor watched this performance with hopeful interest but Dover had too much on his mind to bother about the neurotic behaviour of pregnant women. Having solved the mystery of the murder of Walter Chantry (and, in consequence, that of Mrs Boyle as well) his thoughts were now fully occupied with the mechanics of pulling a fast one on MacGregor. Dover didn't often solve his cases but, when he did, he liked to get the exclusive credit for it. In this particular instance, however, he had another axe to grind. MacGregor needed taking down a peg or two. Dover hadn't forgotten the disgraceful bullying to which he had recently been subjected and he was determined to get his own back. He didn't underestimate the magnitude of the task before him, it not being easy for a detective to arrest a murderer without his closest colleague knowing anything about it. Still, he comforted himself, where there's a will, there's a way.

He began laying the first bricks of a false trail. ' There's a through train back to London in the morning, isn't there?' he asked and enjoyed the look of horror that crossed MacGregor's face.

'We're not leaving, are we, sir?'

'Can't see much point in hanging on here,' said Dover. 'We aren't getting anywhere. Why go on flogging a dead duck?'

'But, sir, we haven't been here more than a couple of days. Mrs Boyle was only killed twelve hours ago. What's the chief constable going to say? What are they going to say at the Yard? Good heavens, sir – this is the sort of think they ask questions about in Parliament!'

'Pshaw!' sniffed Dover. 'My responsibility, isn't it? I'm in charge of the case and in my opinion we've gone as far as we can. We can always reopen the investigation if anything new turns up. I've got to look at this from the wider aspect.'

'The wider aspect, sir?'

'The taxpayers' money, laddie,' exclaimed Dover with a sweet reasonableness calculated to try the patience of a saint. 'It doesn't grow on trees, you know. Now, as soon as we get back, you get hold of old Wheelbarrow and tell him I'll want some transport laid on.'

MacGregor didn't go down without a fight. He spent the remainder of their journey back to the hotel pleading with Dover not to throw in the towel at such a ridiculously early stage. There were dozens of promising avenues still to be explored and scores of stones it might be profitable to turn. Why, they'd hardly scratched the surface of the investigation yet!

Dover, loving every minute of it, turned a pair of large and deaf ears to every argument and then, just in case MacGregor thought such foolhardiness suspicious, grudgingly agreed not to make up his mind finally until the following morning. This was a concession that would keep MacGregor on tenterhooks very nicely.

MacGregor's face showed clearly how worried he was. As Dover's assistant, however unwilling, he knew how liable he was to be judged bungling by association. The top brass at

Scotland Yard were going to go clean through the roof when they found out about this little episode. 'Well, you've no objection to me carrying on with things this afternoon, have you, sir?'

'Not once you've checked the time of that train,' said Dover generously. 'First things first, eh? Mind you, I shan't be taking the afternoon off myself.'

'No, sir?'

Dover shook his head. 'Certainly not! I'll be working right up to the bitter end, like I always do.'

'In your room, sir?'

'In my room,' agreed Dover cheerfully. 'I'm just going to spend a couple of hours sort of going over the case in my mind and having a quiet think. Let's face it, that blighter didn't try to kill me for fun, did he? Oh, I've got the answer somewhere, don't you make any mistake about that! What I've got to do now is let my mind go a complete blank and hope that the clue'll float to the top. Like the cream on the milk,' he added, rather pleased with this picturesque touch.

Or the scum on a duckpond, thought MacGregor bitterly. He glanced at his watch. Eighteen hours, say, before they had to leave. Could he solve the case single-handed in that time? He straightened his back. Why not? With two murders it shouldn't be as difficult as all that. There were shoals of leads they hadn't even begun to check. He'd see if Inspector Stokes had got anywhere with that wire and the screw and then he'd question everybody all over again about their movements at the relevant times and . . .

'I think I'd better have a word with old Wheelbarrow myself,' said Dover whose plans for outwitting MacGregor were now beginning to take shape. 'Just to put him in the picture. Scout round and see if you can find him.'

'You'll see him in your room, sir?'

'Where else, laddie?' Dover knew only too well what unkind thoughts were passing through his sergeant's mind. 'And I don't want you barging in and out every five minutes, either.'

MacGregor could promise that he wouldn't be doing that. 'I shan't disturb you sir.'

Dover gave a warning jerk on the reins. 'What are you going to do?' he asked.

MacGregor was vague. 'Oh, just tidy up a few loose ends, sir. I thought I might go and have a word with those artists. I think you were probably right, sir, and we ought to find out a bit more about their activities. I'd like to know how well they know the interior of the hotel, for instance. Even with a verbal description from Mrs Lickes, I can't see a complete stranger being able to fix that wire up just like that. I mean – how would he know there'd be a crack in the woodwork to stick that screw in? How would he know it was wood there at all? It might have been solid brick and he'd have had to drill a hole and plug it to hold that screw. If I can prove that any of the artists, or the Hoopers for that matter, have never been upstairs in the Blenheim Towers – well, it would whittle the lists of suspects down quite a bit.'

Dover decided he'd nothing to worry about. 'Good idea, laddie!' he said with a smile as false as his teeth. 'You go ahead! Do you good, having to stand on your own feet. I always say that a fellow who doesn't make mistakes doesn't make anything.'

MacGregor innocently attributed this astonishing good nature to the fact that Dover was looking forward to spending the rest of the day in bed. It was a prospect that usually mellowed the old fool. 'I'll ask Mrs Lickes to bring your afternoon tea up, shall I, sir?'

'Yes,' beamed Dover. 'I'll have it at four o'clock. But find Wheelbarrow first. I want to see him right away.'

Twelve

Superintendent Underbarrow proved unexpectedly unco-operative or – as Dover preferred to put it – bloody-minded and chicken-hearted to boot.

'But you can't do it!' spluttered the superintendent, going distinctly pallid round the gills. 'Suppose there's a complaint? You'd be for the high jump. And so,' he added, realizing it was more to the point, 'would I. A good lawyer'd crucify you in court and your bosses'd jump on the little pieces afterwards. No – be sensible – it's just not on.'

'I can see why you never made CID,' said Dover nastily. 'I don't know what it's like collecting car numbers in your little book all day long but, in the plain-clothes branch, you've got to be flexible.'

'Flexible?' exploded Superintendent Underbarrow. 'Bent's the word I'd use. What you're proposing breaks every rule that's ever been written and, in my opinion, it's downright unethical as well.'

Dover raised his eyes in supplication to the heavens. ''Strewth!' he groaned. 'This is murder, mate, not a bloody game of cricket. We've got two stiffs laid out on marble slabs and all you can do is yack on about ethics. Just don't forget' –

he gave Superintendent Underbarrow a sharp poke in the chest to see that he didn't – 'one of those bodies might have been mine.'

'But why involve me?'

'That's what I'm beginning to ask myself,' said Dover sulkily. 'I thought you'd jump at the chance to earn yourself a bit of glory.'

'If this scheme of yours misfires, the only thing either of us will earn is the order of the boot. Look, if you must have a witness – and God only knows why you should – what's wrong with your own sergeant? I should have thought he was the obvious choice.'

Dover slumped down crossly on the bed. Up till now, out of courtesy to Superintendent Underbarrow's superior rank, he had remained standing – and a fat lot of good it had done him. 'All I'm trying to do,' he explained impatiently, 'is catch a multiple murderer before he goes round slaughtering other innocent people. You know what they're like – once they start they never stop. I don't know about you, of course, but I happen to have a very highly developed sense of duty. I don't want it on my conscience if somebody else goes and get themselves bumped off.'

'It's not your purpose I'm objecting to,' protested Superintendent Underbarrow unhappily, 'it's your methods.'

Dover flapped an irritated hand. 'Pitch sticks, doesn't it?' he asked. 'Look, without a bit of improvisation, this joker's going to get clean away with it. What choice have I got but to adjust the odds a bit? Don't tell me you've never fiddled anything!'

'Not like this I haven't!' retorted Superintendent Underbarrow, running a finger round his shirt collar and wondering why it always had to happen to him.

Dover leaned forward persuasively. 'That's why I can't use MacGregor, see? He's young and inexperienced. If it isn't all written down in black and white, he doesn't want to know about it.'

'I don't think I do, either,' muttered the superintendent.

'And he's not loyal, you know,' said Dover bitterly. 'He'd shop me as soon as look at me. Look, all I'm asking for is a fair crack of the whip. Nothing can go wrong. We get 'em in here, I go through my routine and from then on we play it by ear.'

The superintendent shuddered. 'It makes the blood run cold even to think about it. I can kiss my pension goodbye if this ever comes out.'

'But it won't come out!' insisted Dover desperately. 'That's why I want you here instead of MacGregor. You know how to keep your mouth shut.'

'That's very reassuring!'

'It's fireproof, I tell you! If everything goes according to plan and we get a confession, there's two of us to swear on oath that it was obtained all legal and above board.'

'But that would be perjury!'

Dover scowled bleakly at Superintendent Underbarrow. 'It's only perjury when you get found out, you oaf! As long as we both spin the same yarn in the witness box, they can't touch us.'

'But, suppose you don't get a confession. You make your accusation and your threats and everything and the snivelling victim just turns round and spits straight in your eye? What about that, eh? You and me'd find ourselves at the wrong end of an official complaint quicker than you could say knife.'

Dover shook his head gently. Really, it made you wonder what some people had been doing all their lives. Talk about being as pig-ignorant as a new-born babe! 'Then we just cut our losses and just flatly deny that the interview ever took place. Two against one again – see?'

Superintendent Underbarrow did see, only too clearly. The trouble was, though, that he was still tempted. He'd had a pretty dull sort of time in the police, all things considered. Transport and traffic administration were all very well but a man did sometimes yearn for a touch of glamour. Mrs Underbarrow would be thrilled to bits, and so would the kids. And a sensational murder case would liven that old scrapbook up no end, by jingo it would! When this broke it would make the national press for sure, to say nothing of the telly. And him outranking this Scotland Yard chap wouldn't do any harm. If he played his cards properly he ought to be able to collar the lion's share of the kudos and . . . Superintendent Underbarrow drew up a chair. 'What exactly is it I'm supposed to do?'

Dover's ungainly form deflated with relief. At bloody last! 'Nothing,' he said. 'I'll do all the work. I just want you here as a perfectly honest, unbiased, independent witness. We'll cook our story up afterwards when we've seen how things have gone. By the way, I hope you know how to handle yourself if there's any rough stuff? Got a truncheon?'

'I'll borrow one from one of the lads downstairs.'

'You won't, you know!' snorted Dover. 'Use your brains, man! That'd be a dead give-away that we were expecting trouble. No,' – he looked round the room – 'grab that candlestick if there's any sign of a punch-up. And be careful where you use it. Above the hair line or in the kidneys is best, then the marks don't show.' He got up and arranged a couple of chairs in the middle of the room. 'You stay standing by the door. And keep your cap on. It makes it look more official.'

'I think I'll keep my gloves on, too,' said Superintendent Underbarrow, beginning to get into the swing of things, 'so that there won't be any fingerprints if I have to use the candlestick.'

'Good idea!' approved Dover. 'Right! Well, I think we're ready. Wheel 'em up!'

Superintendent Underbarrow didn't care for the sound of this. 'Me?'

'Well, one of us has got to and I can't, can I?'

'Why not?'

'They'd smell a rat.'

'I don't see why. Look, the last thing I want to do is start pulling my rank but I am the senior officer. If I go running around like a blooming messenger . . .'

For once in his life Dover actually opened a door for somebody else. It seemed the easiest way of putting an end to a very unprofitable discussion. 'Get your skates on!' he urged. 'They might be going out for a walk or something and you'll miss 'em.'

Superintendent Underbarrow shrugged his shoulders. Why try to prolong the agony? One might as well take a deep breath, hold one's nose and go in at the deep end. The sooner they started, the sooner this extremely dubious business would be over. Even so, he couldn't resist giving vent to one last feeble protest. 'I still think we ought to find some other way.'

'Oh, don't be so bloody wet!' snapped Dover and gave his colleague such a hearty farewell shove in the back that the Fatal Flight nearly claimed its second victim.

As the superintendent clattered miserably down the stairs Dover had yet another bright idea. Even he realized that the coming interview was going to be somewhat nerve-racking. What he really needed was a good stiff whisky but, in the circumstances, a few fags would be better than nothing. With surprising agility he nipped into MacGregor's room and turned it over with a speed and skill that wouldn't have disgraced a professional burglar. An extensive previous experience and a wide knowledge of human nature didn't go unrewarded. In a matter of minutes he found a fifty tin of very expensive cigarettes which had been cunningly hidden under a spare pair of underpants. They were not the brand, Dover noted sourly, that young MacGregor kept for handing round to his friends. Still, there was no time now for crying over other people's petty meannesses. Pausing only to help himself to a spare box of matches, Dover scuttled back like a thief in the night to his own room.

He'd barely finished coughing over his first mouthful of smoke when he heard the sound of voices and footsteps on the stairs.

This was it.

The door burst open.

'Ah, there you are!' Dover's fat face broke into an unconvincing smile of welcome. 'Come along in! I hope this isn't putting you out at all but I reckoned it was about time you and me had another little chat.' He peered over the newcomer's shoulder. 'Where's your daughter?'

Wing Commander Pile's jaw was set grim and hard. 'I think I informed you before concerning the position with regard to my daughter. It has not changed. Furthermore, I myself do not intend to submit to any further questioning in these highly irregular circumstances. If you wish to interview me, you will do so at a police station and in the presence of my solicitor.'

'Blimey!' said Dover, putting on quite a good act of extreme surprise. 'That's a funny sort of attitude to take, isn't it?' He caught Superintendent Underbarrow's eye and after some elaborate head jerking and eyebrow wiggling got the message over. Very quietly the superintendent closed the door.

'Whether it is funny or not depends entirely upon your sense of humour,' replied Wing Commander Pile, as unbending as ever. 'Frankly, I am not very much concerned with what you think.' He turned round to find the door shut and Superintendent Underbarrow leaning casually but solidly against it. His eyes narrowed as he turned back to address Dover. 'May I ask what you imagine you are playing at?'

'I'm not playing at anything,' said Dover smoothly and twirled a chair round so that he could sit astride it with his arms resting on the back. 'Me, I don't think two murders is a game. You won't either, you know. Twenty years in the nick sewing mailbags ain't no picnic.'

Wing Commander Pile's face softened into a granite smile. 'You are not being so stupid as to accuse me of murder, are you?'

'Yes,' said Dover.

'You must be mad!'

'I'll tell you exactly what happened,' offered Dover obligingly, 'then we'll see how mad I am.'

Wing Commander Pile's eyes flickered uncertainly round the room. 'I refuse to say another word without my solicitor.'

'Very wise,' agreed Dover blandly. 'In your position, I'd do the same. But nobody's asking you to say anything. We just want you to listen, that's all. Why don't you sit down?'

'I prefer to stand, thank you.'

'Suit yourself.' Dover ground out his cigarette stub with his boot and lit himself another. 'We'll take the murder of Walter Chantry first because that's where it all started. Now, Chantry rescues you and your daughter from your house. No argument about that, is there? It's my guess that you'd have liked to have done for him there and then but it was too risky. There were other people beginning to knock about and a dead body on your own doorstep might have led to a few too many awkward questions. Then there was your daughter. You wouldn't have wanted her to be a witness to murder, would you? Apart from anything else, you couldn't rely on her to keep her mouth shut. I know you do your utmost to keep her away from other people but you can't keep guard twenty-four hours a day. Sometimes there's a slip-up. Like this lunch-time with Lickes. So, for the moment, you had to let Chantry go.'

Wing Commander Pile changed his mind. He sat down, calmly crossing his legs and folding his arms. 'What utter nonsense!'

'Your first concern was to get rid of your daughter. Mrs Lickes obliged and brought the girl back to the hotel here. That left you free to go after Chantry. You couldn't afford to wait. Chantry had to be killed either before he'd time to put two and two together or before he'd had the opportunity to tell anybody else that the answer was four. The earthquake had spelt disaster for you, but you're sharp enough to turn disaster into advantages. In all that confusion and upheaval you reckoned you'd got a fair chance of murdering Chantry and getting away with it. And so ' – Dover preened himself – 'you would – if they hadn't sent me down. Bad luck for you, but that's life, isn't it? Right – well – you tell Lickes and the

Hooper lad that you're going back to your house to get some clothes and things before joining in with the rescue work. That gets them out from under your feet and they clear off towards the Sally Gate. Now, the next bit I'm guessing but I reckon you did go back to your house and get some clothes. It would be the sensible thing to do before you went after Chantry. You knew roughly where he'd gone because that son-in-law of his had told you. You followed after him, caught up with him and croaked him. That's where you made your first mistake.'

'Really?' said Wing Commander Pile with a sneer.

'If you'd bashed his head in or held his face down in the mud, nobody would ever have known it was murder, would they? In the conditions after the earthquake, anybody could have had an accident and no questions asked. Just you remember that, laddie, when you get to thinking you're infallible.'

Wing Commander Pile yawned elaborately behind his hand. 'Is this going to take much longer?' he asked.

Dover ignored the interruption. 'As soon as you were satisfied that Chantry was dead, you nipped off double-quick and joined in with the rescue work like any other public-spirited citizen. All you had to do now was act normal and keep quiet. Everything was going your way. The rain kept pouring down so, if you'd left any traces, they'd all be washed away. And then you got a real bonus – the ground you'd left Chantry on started slipping away down the side of the hill in a sea of mud.' Dover shook his head sadly. 'If only you hadn't been such a fool as to strangle him! It was such an amateurish mistake. We'd neither of us be sitting here now if only you'd used your loaf.'

Wing Commander Pile looked annoyed but said nothing.

'So there it is,' said Dover, opening MacGregor's tin of cigarettes again. 'And you made nearly as big a botch-up of killing Mrs Boyle, apart from the fact that you murdered the wrong person. I mean, fancy leaving that wire and the screws for forensic to get their greedy paws on! It may take a bit of time but they'll trace 'em back to you, don't you worry.'

' I doubt it,' said Wing Commander Pile.

' Think you've covered your traces, do you?'

' There are no traces to cover.'

' Don't you kid yourself! With your ham-fisted way of going on, a two-year-old baby'll be able to pin 'em on to you.' Dover leaned forward, sociably exhaling a mouthful of smoke in the wing commander's face. 'Do you know, if I put my mind to it, I could tell you a dozen ways of making somebody trip down those stairs without writing murder in big letters all over it. And I wouldn't have turned that landing light out, either.'

'Wouldn't you?' said Wing Commander Pile indifferently.

''Course not! I'd have found a dud electric light bulb and switched 'em over. 'Strewth, you didn't even try to make it look like an accident.'

' I didn't try to make it look like anything for the simple reason that I had absolutely nothing to do with either the death of my dear friend, Walter Chantry, or of Mrs Boyle. I have, I am afraid, comparatively little knowledge of the law but it is my guess that you would not even obtain a warrant for my arrest on such flimsy grounds. Wild speculation is not evidence – and of this latter commodity you have not so far produced one scrap. If you intend to charge me, go right ahead. I understand one can extract extremely heavy damages from the police in cases of wrongful arrest.'

Superintendent Underbarrow squirmed. What a fool he'd been to let himself get mixed up in this. Pile was keeping as cool as a cucumber. He wasn't going to crack, not in a month of Sundays he wasn't. Superintendent Underbarrow had visions of himself being left holding a very nasty baby indeed.

Dover, on the other hand, was quite unperturbed. Admittedly, he hadn't got Wing Commander Pile grovelling at his feet and begging for mercy but it was early days yet. He confidently anticipated a very different attitude when the going got really dirty. 'So,' he said, cocking his head at Wing Commander Pile, 'you're not prepared to sign a full confession?'

Wing Commander Pile looked back with a perfectly steady gaze and laughed.

'It'd be to your advantage,' insisted Dover. 'Save us raking all that muck up in open court.'

The sardonic twist faded from Wing Commander Pile's lips. Even from behind, a pessimistic Superintendent Underbarrow could tell that Dover had at last struck oil. The wing commander cleared his throat. 'What do you mean?'

'Aw – come off it!' advised Dover with gruesome good humour. 'You must take me for a complete Charlie. You shouldn't have tried to polish me off, you know. In fact, of all the mistakes you've made in your life of crime, I reckon that was your biggest. Started me thinking, you see.'

Wing Commander Pile stood up abruptly. 'I am not going to listen to any more of this.'

Dover grinned unpleasantly. 'No?'

Wing Commander Pile addressed himself to Superintendent Underbarrow. 'Kindly stand aside!'

The superintendent eyed him shrewdly and gave Dover the benefit of what little doubt remained. He glanced at the candlestick to make sure that it was within easy reach and then, slowly and deliberately, shook his head.

'Well, that's that,' said Dover as his hapless victim sat down again. 'Now we can start discussing your motive. We needn't bother our heads about why you had the infernal cheek to try and kill me because that's obvious. You knew it was only a matter of time before I nabbed you so you hadn't much choice.'

Wing Commander Pile gritted his teeth and tried, with decreasing expectation of success, to dominate the interview. 'If it will speed things up at all, I am quite prepared to concede that whoever killed Mr Chantry probably tried to kill you for the reasons you mention. I can only repeat that it was not me.' He looked at his watch. 'My daughter is alone in her room. If anything happens to her, I shall hold you entirely responsible.'

'I've told you you can can bring her up here,' said Dover.

'No!'

'Suit yourself! I shan't be keeping you much longer but, I'm afraid, if you think you're going to be reunited with Miss Pile, you're in for a big disappointment.'

'We'll see about that. So far, all I've heard from you is a lot of vague talk. When are you going to produce some facts?'

Dover began to count on his fingers. 'Fact number one: you murdered Walter Chantry. Fact number two: you murdered him because he was the man who dug you and your daughter out of the ruins of your house.'

'A gesture of gratitude, I suppose?' sneered the wing commander.

'No,' said Dover, refusing to be drawn, 'a gesture of pure self-preservation. If there was one thing Walter Chantry was, it was strait-laced. Everybody says that. Being a chum of yours wouldn't have counted for anything. He'd have done his duty and exposed you without batting an eyelid.'

Wing Commander Pile sat very still. 'I don't understand.'

'I don't know exactly what or how much he saw,' Dover went relentlessly on, 'because we've only got your version of the actual rescue. My guess is that at the very least he saw you in bed with your daughter.'

There was a tense silence, relieved only by the deafening squeak of Superintendent Underbarrow's boots as he leaned expectantly forward.

'Do you realize what you are saying?' In spite of all his efforts, Wing Commander Pile's voice came out cracked and strained.

Dover didn't answer.

Wing Commander Pile tried again. 'You can't prove it.'

'That's better!' said Dover. 'I'm glad we're not going to waste time on any protestations of innocence.' He lit another of MacGregor's cigarettes and once again let the smoke drift into the wing commander's face. Dover never missed the chance of kicking a man when he was down. 'Now, proof!' He dropped the match on the floor. 'Your daughter's bedroom was round at the back of the house, wasn't it? Overlooking Sidle Alley?'

'I refuse to answer any more questions!' shouted Wing Commander Pile with such unexpected violence that both Dover and Superintendent Underbarrow jumped nervously.

'All right, all right!' said Dover, keeping a wary eye on his prey. 'You don't have to say anything. I shall call Mr Lickes as a witness. You stopped him taking his evening exercise along Sidle Alley, didn't you, because you said he was spying on the girl when she was getting undressed. I dare say there are plenty of other people in the village who could swear to where her bedroom was so we shan't have any difficulty there. You get the point, don't you? If your daughter had been in her own room at the time of the earthquake, she'd probably have been killed because that part of the house collapsed immediately and was totally destroyed. As it was, she didn't suffer more than a few scratches and Chantry rescued her from the front of the house. He never went near Sidle Alley because by the time he arrived on the scene all that part was already half-way down the hill. Any comments?'

Wing Commander Pile clenched his hands together to hide their trembling. 'I don't have to explain anything. I deny categorically that what you say is true but, even if it was, it wouldn't prove anything. Linda could have been frightened by the earthquake and run into my room.'

Dover shook his head. 'That won't wash. She wouldn't have had time. The earthquake struck without warning. Everybody says that. Besides, if it was all as innocent and above board as that, what did you kill Chantry for?'

The wing commander was not too distraught to spot the weakness in that particular piece of reasoning. 'But you're arguing in circles!' he protested. 'You say I murdered Mr Chantry because . . . because of what he saw and then you say he must have seen something because I killed him. It's so illogical.'

'It'll do to fix you!' rasped Dover, beginning to get cross.

'I can't believe you're serious. You still haven't produced one single scrap of evidence. I think you're bluffing.'

Superintendent Underbarrow looked anxiously at Dover. The wing commander was proving an uncomfortably tricky customer and it was unnerving to hear him producing exactly the same arguments that the superintendent himself had raised earlier on. The moment had now come for Dover to produce the ace which he was supposed to have up his sleeve. Superintendent Underbarrow, a regular churchgoer and bridge player, offered up a fervent prayer that it wasn't going to be trumped.

Dover was beginning to sweat a bit, too. If he'd realized it was going to be all this trouble, he'd never have started the blooming thing. When you've actually solved a murder case, the least you expect is that the guilty party will chuck his hand in after a decent interval. He glared resentfully at Wing Commander Pile. Oh well, off with the kid gloves. 'You don't think I'd get a conviction?'

'Not in a thousand years!' came the scornful reply.

'So I'll need a confession from you, won't I?'

'I should like to know how you propose to get it. What are we in for now? Brain washing? Torture? Third degree?'

Dover shook his head. 'You're going to give me one. Oh, you will, mate! I've got the whip hand – see? Now, I agree with you. I don't think I've got enough evidence to persuade a jury to convict you of murder.'

'At last!'

'But I reckon I have got just about enough to charge you and bring you to trial.'

Wing Commander Pile frowned. 'What would be the point of that?'

'Oh, come on, laddie! Use your brains! There's more ways of killing a cat than skinning it. I'm going to throw you to the lions. What do you think the newspapers are going to do to you, eh? They'll flay you alive! An ex-officer having it off with his own mentally retarded daughter? 'Strewth, your name'll stink from one end of the country to the other. This may be a permissive society, mate, but there are still some things the Great British Public won't stomach.'

The wing commander shrank visibly from his chair. 'You can't do that,' he muttered.

'And think what they'll do to your daughter,' continued Dover with a ghastly chuckle. 'They'll question her, you know. Ask her if she ever slept in the same bed as daddy, what sort of things he . . .'

'Stop it!' screamed Wing Commander Pile. 'You filthy, disgusting swine!'

'Look who's talking!' jeered Dover. Now that he'd got his man on the run, his only concern was to pile on the pressure. 'People who live in glass houses shouldn't go around calling the pot black. You . . .'

The wing commander clamped his hands over his ears. 'I won't listen!' he moaned. 'I won't listen to another word!'

'You will, you know,' retorted Dover, leaning across and dragging the wing commander's arms down. 'And don't start any of the rough stuff! Mr Wheelbarrow here and me'd love to have an excuse for giving you a going-over, you lousy punk. Besides, I'm offering you a way out, aren't I? **You** wouldn't want to miss that.'

'A way out?' gasped Wing Commander Pile, not sure that he had heard correctly. He clutched at Dover with shaking hands. 'What do you mean, a way out?'

Dover unclasped his hands from his lapels and pushed the wing commander back in his chair. 'I thought that'd interest you!'

'What do I have to do? Just tell me! I'll do anything, I promise you.'

'Just sign a full confession admitting to the murders of Walter Chantry and Mrs Boyle.'

Wing Commander Pile stared at Dover in dismay. 'Oh, no! No, I can't do that! What good would it do?'

'It would get you off the hook, mate. I'm striking a bargain with you. You give me a signed confession and I'll give you a guarantee that the question of motive won't come out in open court.'

Wing Commander Pile gazed from side to side like a trapped animal. 'I don't quite understand.'

'Look, if you plead guilty to Chantry's murder, the court's not going to go digging around just for the hell of it, is it? Give or take the odd word, they'll accept your version of what happened. You can make up some sort of motive if you want. On the other hand, if you plead not guilty, it's no holds barred. We'll come out with the whole sordid story. Your daughter will certainly be questioned and she may even be called as a witness for the prosecution.'

'My God!' groaned Wing Commander Pile. 'Oh, my God!' He buried his face in his hands.

Superintendent Underbarrow stared at the heaving shoulders in front of him and felt rather sick. Poor devil. Whatever he'd done, you couldn't help feeling story for him. It was somehow strangely humiliating to see a man being broken like this. The superintendent cancelled his plans for telling his wife all about the big moment when they caught the Sully Martin murderer.

Dover was lighting yet another cigarette. 'Well, which is it going to be?' he demanded impatiently. 'I haven't all day to hang around here if you have.'

'I'll sign your confession,' whispered Wing Commander Pile.

'Attaboy!' Dover compounded this unfortunate exclamation with a cocky thumbs-up sign of triumph at Superintendent Underbarrow. 'I thought you'd come round to my way of looking at things. Well, never put off till tomorrow what you can do today.' He snapped his fingers in the air. 'Pen and paper!'

It took Superintendent Underbarrow some little time to realize that the gesture and the request had been directed at him. He was understandably furious when comprehension finally dawned. Damn it all, it was about time somebody put this London fellow in his place! Superintendent Underbarrow was about to undertake this delicate task when Wing Commander Pile raised his head and interrupted him.

'I must go downstairs and see that Linda is all right first,' he said in a calmer voice. 'You needn't worry. I shan't try to run away.'

'Wouldn't do you much good if you did,' said Dover airily. 'You'd not get far.'

The wing commander sighed. 'I won't be more than a minute,' he promised, 'and I'll pring a pen and some paper back with me.'

On an imperious nod from Dover, Superintendent Underbarrow stood aside. Wing Commander Pile managed a faint smile of thanks and then, after a moment's hesitation, turned back to Dover. 'It's really not as bad as it sounds, you know,' he said pathetically. 'My wife died when Linda was born and I had to look after her. For seventeen years I've sacrificed everything for her sake – my career, marriage, everything. I took a job abroad. I didn't want everybody sneering and looking down their noses at her and I thought abroad . . . East Africa. We kept ourselves to ourselves as far as the other Europeans were concerned. We had native servants, of course. They were very good. They really loved Linda and it didn't matter to them that she was . . . So nobody bothered us, you see. I'd have stayed out there, of course, but the company I worked for sold out and my health wasn't . . . I'd forgotten how much people live on top of each other back here at home. Always poking and prying and asking impertinent questions. They won't let you alone.' He rubbed his hand wearily across his eyes. 'I'm not complaining, you understand. I'd do it all again just the same if I had to, but you can't say I've been able to lead a normal life, can you? I thought I was entitled to some – well – compensation. And I wasn't being entirely selfish. It was better for Linda this way. It was!' he insisted with a show

197

Thirteen

Superintendent Underbarrow went across and opened the bedroom window. ' Getting a bit stuffy in here,' he said.

Dover hadn't noticed and he didn't care. He stood up, stretched himself and waddled over to the bed. ' People like him ought to be hanged, drawn and quartered.'

Superintendent Underbarrow gazed unseeingly out of the window. ' I suppose so.'

' There's no bleeding suppose about it!' Dover sat down on the edge of the bed. ' Disgusting devil!'

' You still can't help feeling a bit sorry for him,' said Superintendent Underbarrow, still not turning round.

' I can!' snorted Dover, catching the faint hint of criticism. ' He wants stringing up. He has killed two perfectly innocent people, you know.'

' He's still entitled to a fair trial,' said Superintendent Underbarrow, at last voicing what had been worrying him for some time.

Dover reacted angrily. ' He's entitled to damn all! And what's eating you all of a sudden? You knew how I was going to play it.'

' I didn't realize it was going to be quite so cruel,' confessed the superintendent miserably.

'Well, you won't catch me losing any sleep over it. It was the only way to catch him. We haven't a shred of proof, you know that.'

'Our chaps might have turned up something from Mrs Boyle's murder.'

'And pigs might fly!' sniffed Dover. 'Pile's nobody's fool.'

'You said yourself he'd made mistakes. If we'd spent a bit more time looking we might have . . .'

'It's the same difference, isn't it?' snapped Dover. 'We could rupture ourselves and he'd still not get more than a life sentence. Besides,' – he stretched himself out full length with a grunt of contentment – 'I've no intention of passing my declining years scratching around in this crummy little backwater.' He settled his head on the pillows. 'I don't understand you. You drag me down here to solve your blooming murder case and, when I do, all you can do is bitch about it.' He crossed his feet and closed his eyes. 'Some people are never satisfied.'

Superintendent Underbarrow realized that it was no use talking to Dover. They just weren't on the same wavelength.

Dover yawned.

The superintendent glanced round. 'He's taking his time, isn't he?'

Dover sighed, loudly. These perishing amateurs! Always getting into a flap about something. 'He's got a lot to explain, hasn't he?'

'Poor girl! I wonder what on earth's going to happen to her.'

'They'll stick her in an institution,' said Dover with complete indifference. 'She'll be all right. Best place for her. There,' – he propped himself up on one elbow as he caught the sound of footsteps on the stairs – 'he's coming. Told you there was nothing to panic about.'

But it was MacGregor who opened the bedroom door after a discreet tap. 'I'm terribly sorry to bother you, sir, but . . .' He broke off as he caught sight of Superintendent Underbarrow over by the window. 'Oh, I'm sorry sir, I didn't realize . . .' His voice faded out as he tried to work out what was going on now.

It was left to Superintendent Underbarrow to let the cat out of the bag. He had either forgotten or never really appreciated that Dover and his sergeant were not two hearts beating as one. He was too busy recognizing MacGregor as a substitute dog's-body. 'Ah, sergeant,' he said, 'just pop downstairs and see what's keeping Wing Commander Pile, will you?'

MacGregor's ears pricked up. 'Wing Commander Pile, sir?'

'That's right,' said Superintendent Underbarrow before Dover got a chance to shut him up. 'The sooner we get this confession of his down on paper, the better.'

MacGregor stared accusingly at Dover. 'Confession, sir?' he repeated.

'That's right.' Superintendent Underbarrow looked at the two antagonists and hesitated. 'Er – you did know he was the murderer, didn't you?'

'No, sir,' said MacGregor, still glaring at Dover, 'as a matter of fact, I didn't. The chief inspector must have forgotten to tell me.'

'Oh.' Superintendent Underbarrow risked a glance himself at Dover's flabby face and was not comforted by what he saw there. Had he gone and put his foot in it? He realized that MacGregor was still waiting for him to continue. 'Well, it's all over now. Pity you missed it, eh?'

'Missed what sir?'

Superintendent Underbarrow wished MacGregor would look at him when he addressed him. 'Well,' – he tried a carefree sort of laugh which failed miserably – 'missed the showdown, really. Your chief inspector here just confronted Pile with the facts and he – er – eventually broke down and – er – confessed.'

MacGregor broke off his eyeball-to-eyeball confrontation with Dover. 'And you let him go?' he asked incredulously.

Superintendent Underbarrow felt himself going pink. 'Only to get some paper,' he explained, painfully aware of how feeble it sounded. 'We hadn't got any up here, you see. Oh, and he had to have a word with his daughter as well.'

'My God!' said MacGregor. 'Have you both taken leave of your senses? Fancy letting him . . .' He rushed for the door.

'Hot-headed young bugger!' commented Dover bitterly as MacGregor hurtled down the stairs. 'Acts first and thinks after. You should have pinned his ears back for him, speaking to you like that.'

Superintendent Underbarrow was beyond reply. He hurried over to the open door and listened anxiously to MacGregor shouting and hammering on the floor below. After a couple of minutes the frantic calls stopped and MacGregor could be heard bellowing for assistance from the police downstairs. Almost immediately there came the steady pounding of regulation boots.

'I think I'd better go down and see what's happening,' said Superintendent Underbarrow as, after a short whispered conference, shoulders began crashing into and splintering the wood of a door. 'I don't like the sound of this.'

Dover, still lolling on the bed, watched him go. Funny how some people couldn't wait to meet trouble halfway. Disconsolately he rearranged his pillows. He'd been rather fancying playing the leading role at Pile's trial. Ah well, that's the way the cookie crumbles. You can't win 'em all.

It was ten minutes before MacGregor came up to report. He was so upset that he used quite excessive roughness to shake Dover back to consciousness. Wing Commander Pile had cut his daughter's throat with a razor blade, and then his own.

Now Back in Print

Margot Arnold

The complete adventures of Margot Arnold's beloved pair of peripatetic sleuths, Penny Spring and Sir Toby Glendower:

The Cape Cod Caper	*192 pages*	*$ 4.95*
The Catacomb Conspiracy	*260 pages*	*$18.95*
Death of a Voodoo Doll	*220 pages*	*$ 4.95*
Death on the Dragon's Tongue	*224 pages*	*$ 4.95*
Exit Actors, Dying	*176 pages*	*$ 4.95*
Lament for a Lady Laird	*221 pages*	*$ 5.95*
The Menehune Murders	*272 pages*	*$ 5.95*
Toby's Folly (hardcover)	*256 pages*	*$18.95*
Zadock's Treasure	*192 pages*	*$ 4.95*

Joyce Porter

American readers, having faced several lean years deprived of the company of Chief Inspector Wilfred Dover, will rejoice (so to speak) in the reappearance of "the most idle and avaricious policeman in the United Kingdom (and, possibly, the world)." Here is the series that introduced the bane of Scotland Yard and his hapless assistant, Sgt. MacGregor, to international acclaim.

Dover One	*192 pages*	*$ 5.95*
Dover Two	*222 pages*	*$ 4.95*
Dover Three	*192 pages*	*$ 4.95*
Dead Easy for Dover	*176 pages*	*$ 5.95*
Dover and the Unkindest Cut of All	*188 pages*	*$ 5.95*
Dover Beats the Band (hardcover)	*176 pages*	*$17.95*
Dover Goes to Pott	*192 pages*	*$ 5.95*
Dover Strikes Again	*202 pages*	*$ 5.95*

"Meet Detective Chief Inspector Wilfred Dover. He's fat, lazy, a scrounger and the worst detective at Scotland Yard. But you will love him."   —*Manchester Evening News*

Available from bookshops, or by mail from the publisher: The Countryman Press, Box 175, Woodstock, Vermont 05091-0175. Please include $2.50 for shipping your order. Visa or Mastercard orders ($20.00 minimum), call 802-457-1049, 9-5 EST, Monday–Friday.

Available from Foul Play Press

The perennially popular Phoebe Atwood Taylor whose droll "Codfish Sherlock," Asey Mayo, and "Shakespeare lookalike," Leonidas Witherall, have been eliciting guffaws from proper Bostonian Brahmins for over half a century.

Asey Mayo Cape Cod Mysteries

The Annulet of Gilt	*288 pages*	*$5.95*
The Asey Mayo Trio	*256 pages*	*$5.95*
Banbury Bog	*176 pages*	*$4.95*
The Cape Cod Mystery	*192 pages*	*$5.95*
The Criminal C.O.D.	*288 pages*	*$5.95*
The Crimson Patch	*240 pages*	*$5.95*
The Deadly Sunshade	*297 pages*	*$5.95*
Death Lights a Candle	*304 pages*	*$5.95*
Diplomatic Corpse	*256 pages*	*$5.95*
Figure Away	*288 pages*	*$5.95*
Going, Going, Gone	*218 pages*	*$5.95*
The Mystery of the Cape Cod Players	*272 pages*	*$5.95*
The Mystery of the Cape Cod Tavern	*283 pages*	*$5.95*
Octagon House	*304 pages*	*$5.95*
Out of Order	*280 pages*	*$5.95*
The Perennial Boarder	*288 pages*	*$5.95*
Proof of the Pudding	*192 pages*	*$5.95*
Sandbar Sinister	*296 pages*	*$5.95*
Spring Harrowing	*288 pages*	*$5.95*
Three Plots for Asey Mayo	*320 pages*	*$6.95*

"Surely, under whichever pseudonym, Mrs. Taylor is the mystery equivalent of Buster Keaton."   —Dilys Winn

Leonidas Witherall Mysteries (by "Alice Tilton")

Beginning with a Bash	*284 pages*	*$5.95*
File for Record	*287 pages*	*$5.95*
Hollow Chest	*284 pages*	*$5.95*
The Left Leg	*275 pages*	*$5.95*

Available from bookshops, or by mail from the publisher: The Countryman Press, Box 175, Woodstock, Vermont 05091-0175. Please include $2.50 for shipping your order. Visa or Mastercard orders ($20.00 minimum), call 802-457-1049, 9-5 EST, Monday–Friday.